*Books of Merit*

*Pleased to Meet You*

# *Pleased to* MEET YOU

STORIES

## CAROLINE ADDERSON

Thomas Allen Publishers
Toronto

**Library and Archives Canada Cataloguing in Publication**

Adderson, Caroline, 1963–
    Pleased to meet you : stories / Caroline Adderson.

ISBN–10: 0-88762-220-8
ISBN–13: 978-0-88762-220-5

I. Title.
PS8551.D3267P58   2006       C813'.54       C2006-902038-8

Editor: Patrick Crean
Cover and text design: Gordon Robertson

"The Maternity Suite" was originally published in *Best Canadian Short
Stories, 2002.* "Mr. Justice" first appeared in French in *Romans d'une ville:
Vancouver* then in English as a limited edition chapbook by Biblioasis.
"Falling" won second prize in the 2005 CBC Literary Competition
and was published in *En Route.* "Ring Ring" appeared in *Geist,* "Hauska
Tutustua" in *Room of One's Own,* "Knives" in *The New Quarterly,*
and "Spleenless" in *Brick.*

Published by Thomas Allen Publishers,
a division of Thomas Allen & Son Limited,
145 Front Street East, Suite 209,
Toronto, Ontario M5A 1E3 Canada

  **Canada Council
for the Arts**

ONTARIO ARTS COUNCIL
CONSEIL DES ARTS DE L'ONTARIO

The publisher gratefully acknowledges the support of The Ontario Arts
Council for its publishing program.

We acknowledge the support of the Canada Council for the Arts, which last
year invested $20.0 million in writing and publishing throughout Canada.

We acknowledge the Government of Ontario through the Ontario Media
Development Corporation's Ontario Book Initiative.

We acknowledge the financial support of the Government of Canada
through the Book Publishing Industry Development Program (BPIDP)
for our publishing activities.

10 09 08 07 06     2 3 4 5 6

Printed and bound in Canada

For Allison—
reader
friend

# Contents

*Pleased to Meet You*

# *Falling*

Because the underwriter's wife scraped three long stripes of paint off the side of the car while pulling into a stall next to a concrete pillar in an underground parking garage. Normally she used the van, but had taken the car to return the videos specifically because it was easier to park. She was rueful and the underwriter philosophical and the next day she kept the car so she could take it to the autobody shop for an estimate.

Because the underwriter took the bus.

Before he left the house he filled his pockets with change. To the musical accompaniment of loonies and quarters, he walked the three blocks to the stop. After a not unreasonable wait, the bus came and beached itself against the curb and the underwriter got on, lightening his pockets according to the fare schedule on the box.

Because he made the mistake of taking one of the sideways-facing seats you had to forfeit to the elderly and disabled, which then necessitated that he look at every person boarding to see if they fit this category.

Because, when too many of them looked back into the morning face of the underwriter, he lifted his not-enough-coffee-yet gaze instead to the advertisements running above the heads of the passengers across the aisle. *Marsden Business College A Step in the*

*Right Direction Breathe Clear with Claritin Trouble With Your Tax Forms? Help Is on the Way*

The underwriter read the poem. He read it for the same reason he read the advertisements.

Because, initially, he thought it was an advertisement too.

He read it a second time quite differently but found he understood it even less. Intrigued then, he wondered what it, a thing that existed purely for its own sake, not exactly serving the public good, not selling anything either, was even doing on the bus. Did people still write poetry? Evidently. A woman's name was appended to the poem. Didn't she feel exposed? Why not just get on the bus naked and ride it all over town?

Because, while the bus trawled its way downtown, the underwriter kept on reading the poem. He read it fifteen times at least, then got off at his stop and walked the four long blocks to his office.

By then, the poem was gone.

Because he felt the way he might have if his briefcase had been open shedding papers along the way. Except, of course, he couldn't retrace his steps and retrieve the poem. Where did these things go? Is there a void that will really never fill despite all the keys and birthdays and glasses and names, even sometimes of his own children, that are dropped in it? Despairing, he happened then to glance up at the building's towering mirrored sides.

And two lines of the poem came back.

Because he'd just experienced first-hand the transitory nature of memory. Because he was at the age when brain cells die as silently as butterflies in a sudden frost. Because some days he really couldn't get the names of his own kids straight. He muttered the two lines over and over until he was safely inside and up the elevator and in his own office where he could write them down.

His wife called a few hours later to tell him how much it was going to cost to have the side of the car repainted. They discussed whether to bother going through the insurance company and his wife apologized again for damaging the car. She was an admirable woman in so many ways, but hopeless in this one respect, particularly parallel parking, which sometimes sent her circling a block for a quarter hour in search of a double spot.

After he hung up, the underwriter wished he'd thought to read the salvaged lines of the poem to his wife, but felt too foolish to call her back. Instead he summoned the secretary on the pretext of a dictation. She was new to the office, supplied by a temp agency. The underwriter didn't know much about her other than she had rings in her face and knit surreptitiously under her desk. Despite the jokes cracked behind the boardroom's closed doors, the general consensus in the firm was that knitting cancelled out face jewellery.

The secretary came in and took the seat across from him, cardiganned shoulders hunched against the arctic air conditioning, ready with a pad and pen.

"Falling is not so easy as it looks from the ground."

The secretary took it down. She was left-handed.

"We descend, we descend, only to rise skyward to ourselves."

She wrote it as a second sentence, though in the poem they weren't even consecutive lines.

"That's it," the underwriter said when she looked up for more.

He expected some kind of reaction—why? He didn't expect a reaction to a contract amendment or a memo. She closed the pad and stood to go. Disappointed, he got up too and turned to face the floor-to-ceiling windows. Twenty-seven storeys below, the poem was being conveyed through the city on public transit. He thought of celebrations in hot Catholic places where the statue of a saint is hoisted onto believing shoulders and paraded through the streets. Years ago, the underwriter and his wife had honeymooned in Mexico.

"They don't open."

He turned to the secretary. "What?"

She came over and stood beside him and neither said a thing. Then the secretary placed both her hands on the view and leaned into it until her whole body flattened against the smoked glass. *Click* went her eyebrow ring.

"Don't be afraid," she said.

The underwriter's palms were wet. They left ghosts of themselves on the glass. He moved closer, pressing a cheek against the cool surface, afraid indeed—to look down, to test the pane with his weight.

Finally, he let himself go.

Because the windows were sealed and the poem perfectly safe.

"It'll be ready on Thursday," said the underwriter's wife at dinner.

"Fine."

"You'll have to take the bus again."

There was no question; his wife drove the kids to school. After school, she drove the older boy to soccer and the younger to the pool and in between she ran a home-based business making lampshades for which she needed the van for deliveries and to pick up materials.

"I don't mind," the underwriter said.

"You are too good." She leaned over and kissed him and was catcalled for it by their sons who were twelve and ten and hostile to love though still very much in need of it. The underwriter remembered how it felt to be a boy. The older one, who understood about sex now, was at that age when the thought of intercourse between his parents was revolting. The underwriter laughed and wondered if he was going to have intercourse with the mother of his sons tonight or would she be too tired, who could blame her?

Because that night she climbed into bed smelling of face cream and immediately shut off the light rather than forcing herself to read because she was always the one in her book club who hadn't finished the book.

"I put my thing in," she said.

The underwriter pulled her on top of him and nuzzled her breasts. He used his thumb until she warmed up, then flipped her onto her back. At the moment of her climax, he whispered in her ear, "We descend, we descend . . ."

"Oh!" she cried out. "Oh!"

The second day he took the bus, the underwriter's wife stopped bellowing to the boys to get out of bed and came to the door to say goodbye. "What was that you said to me last night?"

"A line from a poem."

"A poem!" Delight erased a decade off her face. He would have pulled her to him and recited it again right there in the hall, but he didn't want to miss the bus.

Because he was anxious to copy down the rest of the poem.

He looked for it as soon as he boarded.

"Where is what?" the driver asked.

"Yesterday there was a poem."

"Not on this bus."

He did a reckless thing then. He pulled the cord and got off at the next stop with the paper tongue of the transfer in his hand. Ten minutes later another poemless bus came.

It wasn't important, he decided. It wasn't the end of the world. Life would go on. On it would go.

He was late for work. When he came in, the secretary smiled at him because of what had happened the day before. He hurried past, closed his office door, laid his head on the desk. *Milk, eggs, hot dog buns Breathe Clear with Claritin You and your means the person(s) Insured on the Declarations page and, while living in the same household, his or her wife or husband, the relatives of either and Puppy Chow, for a full year, till he's full-grown!*

Because his mind teemed with words.

Because he had two lines and not a syllable more.

That night the underwriter fell. He'd been standing at his office window working up the nerve to lean. Too late, he discovered the glass had been removed. Down he tumbled, yet it was not the terrifying sensation he'd assumed. He actually enjoyed the wind on his face and the attention gravity paid him, so confident was he that, somewhere below, the poem was there to break his fall.

He woke to the sound of crying. Beside him his wife lay deafened by orange foam earplugs.

"Daddy!"

He leapt out of bed and followed his son's cries down the hall. It was his younger boy, the ten-year-old, whom they couldn't in all fairness forbid to play the computer games his older brother was allowed. The underwriter sat on the bed and, taking the trembling boy in his arms, kissed his forehead and rocked him, as though he were a baby. Even as he was comforting the boy, he envied him his cartoon nemeses, masked and bazookaed villains, dog-headed monsters, zeros and ones on a chip. All day the underwriter had fought off adult demons—loss, disappointment, futility. He was not normally a moody person. His wife had given him a look over dinner in response to some curt thing he'd said. Probably she was wondering what had happened to the great lover of the night before.

"Shh," said the underwriter. "Shh."

He remembered pacing at night with his son when he was just a few weeks old and colicky, his angry baby fists waving. All at once an image came to him—what the secretary was knitting under her desk.

A tiny blue mitten.

"Falling is not so easy as it looks from the ground," whispered the underwriter to his son, who instantly stopped crying to say, "Wha?"

"It lies there on the snow, small thing—" He strained. "—small thing, all we have ever lost."

The boy sniffed loudly and relaxed in the underwriter's arms.

"We descend, we descend . . ."

He kept repeating the three lines over and over until the boy fell back to sleep.

The underwriter drove to work the next day. He stopped at the secretary's desk when he got in, in case he'd seemed rude the day before. She was knitting openly now. No one cared as long as she answered the phone. "What are you making?" he asked.

"A scarf." She lifted it to show him, a long orange swath.

"You finished the mittens."

"What?"

"Weren't you knitting mittens yesterday?"

"God no. I'm just a beginner."

The underwriter stared at her, then walked off shaking his head.

Because he was in a much better frame of mind today. The night before, sitting in his son's room waiting for his breathing to deepen to the point of no return, he'd remembered the name of the poet. It was an easy name for him, his wife's middle name in fact, grafted onto a revered former prime minister's. On his lunch break he walked to a big downtown bookstore.

Because he found nothing by that author.

"I can order it for you," the clerk said.

Because, walking back to the office, he decided to phone the poet. His hands grew clammy. The poet was a woman, true, but it wasn't going to be that kind of call. Still, the underwriter felt disloyal, as he had the day before yesterday standing at the window with the secretary. He remembered how easy his wife had made it for him all those years ago. He'd been in love with someone else and rejected. How grateful he was for how his life had turned out.

Last year the underwriter's wife had discovered a lump in her breast, but it had been, thank God, benign.

The secretary was still at lunch when he got back to the office. He opened her desk drawer and took the phone book out from under a ball of orange wool.

His wife sounded breathless when she answered, likely from running up the basement stairs. Her workroom was down there.

"Did one of the kids ever lose a mitten?"

"Probably." She didn't sound annoyed until he told her that he loved her. "What is going on?" she cried.

While he was reassuring his wife that everything was fine, he looked the poet up in the phone book.

His wife said, "You've been working too hard." She said, "I'd like you to see a doctor."

There were several listings with the same initial. He picked, wrongly, the one paired with what he imagined was a poet's address. On the second try a woman answered. He said her name and she responded. He said, "The poet?" and she laughed. "Ye-es. Who's this?"

He'd expected a different voice, a wounded voice, a voice raw and wise. She sounded like a teenaged girl. He was less nervous now.

"I read your poem on the bus."

"Really?"

"Yes."

"And?"

"I only remember three of the lines. I was hoping you could read it to me. I'd like to write it down." He had a pen in hand, a piece of paper ready.

"Get away," she said. "Who is this?"

"Really."

"Okay then. What three lines do you remember?"

He told them to her.

"Say the last one again," she said.

"It lies there on the snow, small thing, all we have ever lost."

"Hey. That's good."

"No. That's all I remember."

"I mean the line is good."

The underwriter scratched his confused head. "That's not what you wrote?"

After he finished talking to the poet, he sat at his desk jotting notes so he wouldn't forget.

Because I remember how it felt to be a boy.

Because, the first time, her breasts smelled like vanilla.

Because I went out walking that heartbroken winter and found a mitten in the snow.

*With thanks to Elizabeth Brewster*

# Petit Mal

First the pentagram. It preoccupies Inge all day. Then out of the blue she remembers the girls. In the middle of Seniors' Aquafit. In her mind's eye they rise out of the crystal and chlorinated waters of the Kerrisdale pool while Denise, the instructor, calls out, "Small circles, small circles!" and bops in the water with them to Tommy Dorsey.

"Now travel back! Travel back!"

There were two of them, Inge remembers as she travels back. Nine or ten years old, dressed alike in knee socks and shorts and sleeveless blouses knotted at the midriff. One had sandy ponytails like spaniel ears, the way Inge used to do her daughter Lisa's hair. The other girl was dark and wore barrettes. Both were thin, the lighter one taller. Being older, they weren't friends of Lisa, but they went to Elm Park Elementary too, and Lisa knew their names. Lisa was in grade two. Wallace was only in kindergarten, which means this happened thirty-five years ago.

In the pool directly in front of Inge is a woman with ash-flavoured cotton candy for hair. She seems to have fallen asleep in the chest-deep water, poor soul. She's not moving at all.

Denise: "Knees up! One, two, three, four!"

Inge marches under water.

After class Inge showers in the tiled room. There are no individual stalls. Most of the women shower in their bathing suits, though a few, like Inge, are not so modest. "I saw you at the symphony," someone says.

The water is running in Inge's ears and she's straining for concrete facts: names, the street they lived on. Is it possible she sent Lisa and Wallace away with the girls without even asking where?

"Yoo-hoo?" the woman says.

Inge comes to, sees deflated breasts, a broad white Caesarean scar. The woman's voice booms: "Was that your son you were with?"

Inge, assuming hearing difficulties, nods.

The woman turns to rinse her front, shouting over her shoulder now. "I didn't think much of the concert. I don't like that flowery music. I prefer the Pops. Something you can hum along to."

Inge recognizes her now by the flaps of mottled skin over her shoulder blades. Useless fins. The one who fell asleep in class. Inge turns the shower off, wrings out her suit then gives the chatty woman a polite smile as she heads for the change room.

A minute later the woman joins her, towelling herself and picking up the too-loud conversation where it left off. She raises a sizable pair of nylon underpants at arm's length. "I told the friend who brought me, 'There's that elegant lady from Aquafit.' I said I thought it was nice that your son would give up a Sunday afternoon to go to the symphony with his old mom. If it was your son, that is. He could have been your boyfriend."

"Hardly." Inge steps into her mules and hastens for the dryers.

"Why not? The things people get up to these days."

The hot blasting air is a short-lived refuge. Inge's cropped hair dries before the machine shuts off.

Her name is Sheila, she tells Inge after she has followed her to the bathroom. Toilet paper sticks to the wet floor like bleached

entrails tossed down to be read. Sheila looks at it. "Disgusting! Is
your son married?"

They stand before the mirror, Inge a head taller. Sheila pulls a
cotton turban over her damp grey, plucks free a fringe at her forehead. Inge puts on her earrings, feeling for the holes. If she refuses
to answer these nosy questions, next week will be strained. She
enjoys the class very much. She always sleeps well on Wednesday
night.

She settles on: "No. He isn't married."

"He's good-looking. What does he do?"

"He's a tax lawyer."

Sheila leans over the counter, closer to the mirror, and blues
her transparent lids. "I have a daughter. She's a social worker."

Inge is even about to offer up additional information for friendly
good measure—she has a daughter too—when an explosive report
from the bathroom stall behind interrupts her.

Sheila cries, "I'm not going to stand here and listen to that!"
She snatches up her cosmetic bag and sails indignantly out, leaving
behind a relieved Inge.


Back home Inge gets started on dinner, slicing cabbage on the
board then tipping the purple shreds into the pot. The salt shaker
is almost empty. When she goes to refill it she finds a Sifto box of
air. This gives her pause—since when would she put an empty box
back in the cupboard? And she shivers, like she did this morning
when she saw the pentagram.

Five sharp points embedded in a circle.

Quickly, she pushed the box back under the bed.

She wears her white hair very short, shaved at the nape. The
stubble reared. All over her bare arms the follicles puckered. She
stayed kneeling on the carpet for several minutes. But why? She's
not religious. Her upbringing was entirely secular. She was born
in 1933, in Heideman, near Dresden, to a German mother and a

British father who had the good sense to take his family home as soon as he smelled what was on the wind. Technically she's Jewish, because her mother was, technically, though Inge has never crossed the threshold of a synagogue. For her own also technically Jewish children she provided the usual neutered symbols: Christmas trees, Easter eggs.

Despite all this. Even though, if pressed to reveal something so personal, she would say atheist. Notwithstanding the fact that she isn't superstitious in the least. Present her with a ladder and she will walk right under it to prove it! Really, she doesn't believe in a malignant supernatural being—Satan, Beelzebub, Who-have-you. The Devil didn't make the Nazis do it.

She's worried, very worried about her son.

Alone, Inge would be happy with a green salad, or cottage cheese and an apple. Or she'd make soup on Sunday and eat it every night for a week, Saturday directly out of the pot. But now that Wallace has come home, she's succumbed to a maternal compulsion to nourish her child. Sometimes Wallace works late or goes out after work so isn't even there to eat. She doesn't ask him to call her on these occasions. She wants him to feel free to come and go as he likes.

When he is there for dinner, it's almost worse. He never mentions Nicole, his "partner." Inge phoned Nicole last week and assured her she would always consider her family. In actual fact, Nicole and Wallace haven't been married long enough for Inge to take her daughter-in-law into her heart, though she likes her well enough. Is there any hope of reconciling? Inge expects not and didn't ask. When they couldn't even refer to each other as husband and wife? She sighs. So much for passion.

There is this painful unbroached subject, and now there is another. Tonight the meal is made worse—excruciating for Inge—by the pentagrammed box under Wallace's bed downstairs.

"How was your day?"

When Wallace looks up, Inge sees what that kooky Sheila saw—a face that could launch a thousand biddies across the deep end on flutter boards. Smooth jaw, tidy haircut. She can still see her baby in his face. He's also something of a comedian, a quality that aggrieves her now that she knows he's in trouble. She'd like straight answers to the questions she can't ask. What Inge would do to get a little of her howler back.

"I've got a case at the moment," Wallace tells her, "a guy who's gone twenty-three years without paying taxes."

"My goodness. How did he get away with that?"

Wallace shrugs. "He just never filed. What did you do today, Mom?"

"I went to Aquafit. I'll sleep like a baby tonight. How's the pork chop?"

"Pork chop. Pork chop."

"Have more cabbage. I know you like it."

Wallace forks in the last of it. He looks at his watch. "Mom. I've got a meeting."

"A meeting?" Cloaked figures spring into her head. The moon rises, full and red. "There's strudel!"

As though dessert could save him.

Wallace gets up from the table. "Please, Mom. Just go on as you usually do. Pretend I'm not here. Hopefully, I'll be out of your hair in a few months."

Inge cups both sides of her head. "You're not in my hair."

He disappears down the basement stairs to his old room. As a teenager he used to pound down the second he could escape the table. A minute later the music would start. Inge didn't think of it as music at the time, but compared with today—at least they played instruments. At least they *sang*. This was the reason she put him in the basement, to spare herself and Lisa. In those days his cave was postered with ghoulish characters, white faces, tarred eye sockets, tongues protruding. There was one, a man with a woman's name. Another parent told Inge he bit the heads off live chickens during his concerts. "He's *diabolical*," the woman had said.

Inge is rinsing the dishes and loading them in the dishwasher when Wallace comes back up. He's in a T-shirt and jeans, carrying his father's old briefcase, much larger than the one he uses for work. Inge feels queasy wondering what's in it.

"Will you be late?"

"Probably." He offers her a hug. "I'll want strudel when I get back. If anyone comes to the door, don't answer. Particularly if they're holding an empty plate."

Alice. That was his name. And oh! Shudder! She's just remembered another: Black Sabbath!

*I will not go down,* Inge tells herself. *I will not look in that box.*

Those girls. That was the start of it, she's sure. Why else would they suddenly pop into her head after all these years?

Ponytails. Knee socks. Bunny barrettes.

Nowadays ten-year-old girls do not dress like that. They wear vinyl miniskirts and platform shoes and teeny tops that stop short of their belly buttons. They probably wear thong underpants. Inge has seen her share of the thong at the Kerrisdale pool, vast pale buttocks separated by a string. What is the point? Today's ten-year-old wears the lip gloss and cross earrings and temporary tattoos her older granddaughter in Calgary expressed a fervent wish for over the telephone when asked what she wanted for her birthday. "Do you let her wear those things?" Inge asked. Lisa said, "How can I stop her?"

The girls who rang Inge's doorbell were innocently dressed. The picture of sweetness. When Inge answered, they quickly showed teeth too big for their mouths.

"Yes?" Inge said, discounting cookies, because they were in street clothes.

The girls introduced themselves; Inge does not remember their names. "We're starting a Sunday school," said the one with spaniel ears. "We want to know if Lisa and Wallace want to come."

"But it's going to be on Saturday," said the dark-haired girl with barrettes. "Because we have real Sunday school on Sunday."

Inge smiled. "Saturday school?" Then Lisa appeared and pushed her way out, awed and disbelieving she could be so lucky as to receive these two on her porch. The girls explained about the Saturday-Sunday school. It was to be held in the basement of the ponytailed girl's house. They would round the children up and lead them there themselves. It would last half an hour. Bible stories, songs, games. They would bring them all home again.

Lisa clutched Inge's arm and jumped up and down.

"I'll have to speak to your mothers about it," Inge hopes she said.

On Saturday morning the girls returned for Lisa. Inge had decided to allow her to go. Why not let Lisa decide for herself what she believed? She would come home with questions they could talk about. But when she and Wallace came out on the porch to wave goodbye, Wallace saw the three children waiting on the sidewalk with the dark-haired girl while the ponytailed one escorted Lisa down the walk. Naturally, he wanted to go too. Inge hustled him back inside to receive his planned dose of undivided attention—the other reason she'd let Lisa go. He wouldn't have it. He threw himself down, screaming and rolling on the floor as though his clothes were on fire. Inge settled resignedly on the bottom stair, helpless to intervene until his rage was exorcised. When he got like this she used to wonder, jokingly of course, if he wasn't possessed.

After Wallace leaves for his meeting, Inge goes directly downstairs to his room. It's decorated now with a yellow flower-print comforter and matching shams, for when her granddaughters come to visit. Instead of ghouls, Renoir girls in impractical dresses flounce across the walls. The first thing Inge did when Wallace moved back was take Lisa's old dolls and stuffed toys that lined the shelves and repack them in the cedar trunk.

She creaks down onto her knees, feels around under the bed-skirt. Sliding the box out, she can tell it's lighter than when she struck it with the vacuum nozzle this morning. A white box with reinforced corners. Inge saw these same boxes the last time she was at Ikea. They come in various sizes. This one is about six inches deep, ten inches wide and eighteen inches long. It looks like he traced around a bowl with a black marker to make the circle then used a ruler for the star.

Her son, the artist.

She jostles the box. Something inside slides back and forth.

Open the lid.

If she does, she'll turn into a different kind of mother from the one who averted her eyes as she stripped and balled his tacky sheets, who, after she'd done the wash, returned the Baggie to his jacket pocket and the condom to his jeans. Who never said a thing.

Inside is another box, rectangular, stamped *Made in China*.

Candles.

Eyes stinging with relief, Inge pulls off the lid.

Salt.

She remembers the Sifto box she crushed before dinner. Twisted off the metal spout, dropped the box on the floor and stamped it flat so it wouldn't take up so much space in the recycling bag.

She pokes a tentative finger in. Burrows to her middle knuckle. Her finger hooks on something. She pulls.

The handle is bone, the blade silver.

Despite Aquafit, she does not sleep well that night. Every time the house talks in its sleep, Inge sits up and listens. She gets out of bed and looks out the window to see if Wallace's car is there yet.

The rest of the week Inge is fretful and distracted, even though Wallace stays home and works, except Saturday, when he goes to a movie with a friend. She believes him. Why shouldn't she? She doesn't enter his room, not even to clean it. *Salt* tops the shopping list. Two separate trips to the store and both times she forgets. She thinks about calling Lisa but she wouldn't be able to say what's really troubling her apart from the dissolved marriage. She respects Wallace's privacy.

What every mother wonders: is this my fault? How remiss has she actually been, how negligent, how blind? This business with the girls: how could she have let it go on for so long? And were there other signs, incidents at school, for example, that no one told her about?

Every time the girls brought Wallace and Lisa home, Inge quizzed them about what they'd done at Saturday school. They each had a picture they'd drawn and Inge could generally figure out Wallace's by looking at Lisa's. Jesus walking on water. The miracle of the loaves and fishes.

"What do you make of all this?" Inge asked them, but they seemed to have no opinion. Apparently the girls used a felt board when they told stories. Wallace liked how, afterward, he was allowed to stick the people and animals on upside down.

Aquafit would have been a relief if it weren't for Sheila. But when Inge gets into the pool she sees so many old people she wonders if Denise can keep track of them all. Would she notice if one, succumbing, slipped below the surface, or would she keep on calling out, "Hop, hop, hop!"? The rest of them can hardly be depended on. Eyeglasses spattered with water droplets or left in lockers, they're practically blind. Sheila is in the front row. Inge stations herself at the back.

After class Inge stays in the near-empty pool and backstrokes a few lengths. Without the piped music, she finds it peaceful and relaxing to glide along watching the light off the water crinkle an aurora across the domed ceiling. For the first time since she opened the box, her anxiety subsides enough to allow for rational thought. There is such a thing as evil, no one could deny it, but is Wallace involved in it? She passes under the string of coloured flags, straightening her arms to break the impact.

On the homeward length an idea, gestated in her confusing week, is finally born. There are *two* kinds of evil. Inge borrows names for them from her nursing days: petit and grand mal. Grand mal evil makes the news, makes history. Petit mal is personal, insidious. The Nazis were grand mal. The girls on the porch— petit mal.

And Wallace?

The shower room is empty. Nor is Sheila among those still in the change room. The pool is part of the community centre, which also houses the library where Inge goes today once she's dry and dressed. There must be a book that could help a person in her predicament, but as she passes through the clicking detector she realizes she won't be able to approach the librarian and request it. Old men sit at the tables reading newspapers or tomes about the war. Always the war. People line up to use the computers. Inge doesn't know how.

The encyclopedias live together in one section of shelf. Inge uses two hands to pull out *S* of the *Britannica*.

"Boo!"

She slams it with a start. There is Sheila in her turban, some kind of witch materializing stoutly to fill half the aisle. "How's that gorgeous son of yours?"

Inge cringes at the over-loud voice. Sheila hasn't even met Wallace, for heaven's sake. She clapped eyes on him once. He's not the boy next door. Even as she's thinking this, it occurs to Inge that she knows what Sheila looks like naked, where she's scarred and where she sags—*and* vice versa. Immediately she wishes they didn't share so intimate a knowledge.

"How old is he? He looks so young."

Inge turns to fill the crevasse made by the extracted volume, showing Sheila her rigid back. "He's forty."

"My daughter is thirty-six. She isn't married either."

It is only this second, hearing this telltale comment, that Inge realizes Sheila is matchmaking. That Sheila is Jewish. Now it all makes sense. Inge softens at the same time something inside her twists. Coiled in her every cell, the guilt of a survivor.

"Come to my place for tea," Sheila says.

"I can't. I've got to get home and get dinner on."

"I'm divorced," Sheila says.

"I'm cooking for Wallace. My son. I'm widowed."

"And he comes over and eats dinner with his mother!" Sheila raises her ringed hands in the air and shakes them, as though to say, *Oy, oy, oy.* "Off you go. But you'll come tomorrow? Here." She yanks her purse off her hip, plunges into its overstuffed depths. "I'll write down the address."

And Inge can't say no.

She phones Lisa when she gets home. Inge thinks: this is what a daughter is for. A son you baby. A daughter you confide in. "About your brother," she says after the pleasantries. Your brother and the Prince of Darkness.

"Is he still there? Oh my God."

"When did you talk to him last?"

"A few weeks ago. Is he even looking for a place?"

"How did he sound to you?"

"Fine," Lisa says. "Maybe *too* fine. I mean, if Barry kicked me out, I'd jump off a bridge."

"No you wouldn't."

"You're right. I've got the girls. I'd threaten to!"

"Did she kick him out?" Inge asks.

"I assume so—"

Inge hears a plaintive voice in the background, her younger granddaughter. "I'm talking to Oma," Lisa tells her. "I'll be there in a second." To Inge she says, "Does he seem depressed?"

"Depressed? No. It's just—I worry."

"That's your job."

Inge wants to ask her about the Saturday-Sunday school. Does she remember? What really happened? The extension clicks and mouth breathing fills the line.

"Erin?" Lisa says.

"Oma!" the little one screams.

Sheila is still lifting the newspapers and the opened and unopened mail stacked all over her sideboard. She looks taller dry, hair teased high and crisped with spray, a wasps' nest. "What's your last name, Inge?"

"Brenner."

"And you've lived in the neighbourhood long?"

"Almost forty years. I'm on Forty-fifth. Just down from the church. The green house."

"It's gone downhill, I'm sure."

"No. Not at all."

"I've never seen so many Chinese!"

Denise, their Aquafit instructor, is Chinese and probably born in Vancouver. Inge states the obvious. "I'm an immigrant myself."

"I can't find it, damn it."

"What are you looking for?"

"A paper. Since you're here I was going to ask you to do me a favour. Forget it. I'll get the kettle on."

She leaves Inge at the table. It's as disorganized as the sideboard, and Inge wonders if she should clear a place to set the teapot. "How long have you lived here?" she asks.

"Six months," Sheila calls through the pass-through window.

Inge thinks of that term she keeps hearing on the CBC: *down-sized*. Sheila has apparently moved the entire contents of her house into this one-bedroom apartment. In the corner a wicker chair leans against the wall. It's supposed to hang from the ceiling by a chain like a birdcage. Lisa used to have one. Such clutter. The woman is a pack rat.

"Where were you before?"

"Peterborough. I wanted to be closer to my daughter."

When she comes back, Inge notes that Sheila's taste in clothes runs along the lines of her taste in upholstery—big floral prints. "These are diabetic cookies." She sets the plate down on the *Crossword Digest* and smiles at Inge with front teeth outlined in gold. Inge supposes they'll be planning the wedding this afternoon. Maybe they'll get as far as naming the grandchildren.

"Do you have a picture of your daughter?"

"A whole boxful. I'm not in any hurry to unpack it."

Before Inge can ask what she means, the phone rings on the table in the hall. "Coming! I'm coming! Hello? *Ahh!*" Sheila slams the receiver down.

"Who was it?" asks a startled Inge.

"The Devil."

A vein in Inge's temple begins to throb. She stares at Sheila marching back to the kitchen to unplug the screaming kettle. Over the glug of the teapot being filled, the ceramic clink of the lid, Sheila explains, "That library computer. It sounds like Satan himself. My book is in."

She carries in a tray. "It's the latest Stephen King. I just love him. As if life isn't horrible enough, eh? Just throw that stuff on the couch. What a damn mess." She waits while Inge gathers up the newspaper sections, the flyers with the coupons cut out, and sets them neatly on the arm of the couch. Sheila unloads the tray then pulls her chair in under herself, shifting hen-like on the seat. "Here. Go ahead. Fix it the way you like. I don't have real sugar."

"I don't take it."

"So tell me all about Wallace. What's he like?"

Inge rubs a tiny circle over the pain. "He's wonderful. A very considerate son. He has a good job."

"You're lucky."

"Yes. But you still worry, don't you?"

Sheila reaches for a cookie, gesturing that Inge should help herself too. "What are you worried about?"

"He's an adult, of course. I'm not responsible anymore for his happiness or his safety."

Crumbs cling to Sheila's bright lipstick. "He's unhappy?"

"I don't know. I just worry. What if he is? Is it my fault? Is it because of mistakes I made?"

Sheila, holding a crescent of cookie in her teeth, lifts the teapot with both hands. "What mother hasn't made mistakes?" She showers Inge in crumbs. But the relief Inge feels just hearing Sheila say this makes her glad she came. This is what she really needs, someone impartial to talk to. She fills her own mug. *World's Greatest Nag*.

Sheila dumps an envelope of sweetener in hers. "Have you got a headache?"

"It's nothing." Inge waves it off. "You know, I even feel responsible for his character. Isn't that silly?"

"What's the matter with him? He sounds like a dream."

"He always was a good boy, but sensitive. The type that can easily fall in with the wrong people. His father died when he was hardly more than a baby."

"Did you kill him?"

Inge stiffens. "Pardon me?"

"Is it your fault his father died?"

"No. Of course not. It was a work accident."

"Then what are you so guilty about?"

Inge adds milk to her tea, makes a whirlpool with the spoon. Though Sheila talks sense, Inge finds, once again, that she doesn't care for the way she talks it.

"Where does he live?" Sheila asks.

The tea tastes dusty. Inge wonders how old it is. "He's with me at the moment. Things didn't work out with his partner."

"Ah," says Sheila with the look of someone who has just won a bet. "That's what I thought. A good-looking, clean-cut boy. Takes his old mom to the symphony. Lives with her."

"He's looking for his own place."

"I wouldn't mind having a son like that. I really wouldn't." Sheila flaps her wrist. "Oo-la-la!"

Inge stares. Sheila thinks Wallace is a homosexual? "He *was* married," she hastens to add.

"I just don't like those mannish haircuts on the women. And they're so angry all the time."

"Who?"

"The lesbians. I saw one the other day. You won't believe this." Sheila leans forward, relishing the detail. "She actually had a *beard*."

The conversation has taken so ridiculous a turn, Inge starts to laugh, but to her dismay, tears come fast behind. "Excuse me," she says. "Where is your . . . ?"

Sheila, looking baffled, points down the hall.

Inge negotiates the obstacle course of furniture. In the bathroom, she splashes cold water on her embarrassed face then dries it with the monogrammed guest towel in the basket next to the basin. Under the towel is a trove of old motel soaps, brought from Peterborough by the look of them. Lack of sleep. That's Inge's trouble. If she could get a good night's sleep she wouldn't feel so distraught. She sits on the toilet and closes her eyes. When she opens them, she sees an index card taped above the tissue roll. Without her glasses, she can only make out the larger print of the title: *Prayer For Cancer Patients*. How odd, thinks Inge. Sheila prays while she's going to the toilet.

She turns on the tap again to wash her hands, still puzzled. If Sheila isn't Jewish—and even if she is, so what?

"What's the matter with you? Are you having a breakdown or something?" Sheila asks when Inge returns to retrieve her purse and excuse herself.

"It's *stress*." Another CBC word. "I'm sorry to leave like this. I need a lie-down."

Sheila follows her to the door. "Should I call a cab?"

"No. I'm three blocks away. I'll be all right. Thank you for tea."

"He doesn't have AIDS, does he?"

"Oh!" Inge claps a hand over her mouth. "I hope not!"

Only now, at the mention of disease, does the prayer taped on the bathroom wall register. Sheila, the poor woman—she's ill. Even as Inge is attempting escape, she feels compelled to say something kind. "We didn't get the chance to talk about your daughter. We'll have to do that next time."

An actual physical change takes place in Sheila. Genie-like, she seems to swell. The flowers on her blouse grow and open. "She wants me to accept her. Fine, I say. I accept you. But I don't accept *her*. A big fat mama with chains hanging off her. None of them shave. It turns my stomach."

Inge withers in Sheila's wind. She draws her purse to her chest. Sheila's hand is still on the doorknob, tight.

"I had no idea this is what she came out here for. I moved here to be closer to her and now she won't speak to me. She won't speak to me until I accept her situation. What she really wants is for me to *approve*. Well, I don't. I'm sure you feel the same about your son."

Inge presses her temple.

"You love him, but you can't deny you'd much rather he found a nice girl to give you a grandchild before you die. I knew you'd understand."

Sheila opens the door and points Inge into the hall.

Inge says, "I'll see you at Aquafit, Sheila."

It must have been the second or third Saturday of Saturday school that Inge woke to the sound of crying. She found Wallace backed into the corner of his bed behind a defensive wall of covers. "I'm scared," he said.

"Of what?"

He couldn't say. If it was a dream, it defied description. She got him settled and went back to bed, was just slipping into unconsciousness when he cried out again. It had been four years since she'd slept with another person. She was accustomed to a queen's space. Wallace thrashed. His teeth crunched gravel. He stayed with her till Wednesday.

On Saturday morning, as Inge was divvying up the pancakes between their three plates, Wallace asked, "Where's Daddy?"

"He's dead," Lisa said.

"Can he talk to me?"

"No," said Inge. "But you can talk to him."

"See?" Wallace told Lisa.

The doorbell rang—the girls coming to collect them. Wallace shrank down.

Lisa said, "You're a baby, Wallace."

"I am not!" He slid off his chair and ran to open the door.

And still Inge didn't put two and two together. Not that night when Wallace whimpered as she shut off the light, or later when his shrieks cut the night.

"What is wrong? What are you afraid of?"

He held his whole body stiff.

When she saw them off the next Saturday, Wallace looked back over his shoulder at her. She'd seen just that look—hollow, imploring—somewhere before.

Even so. Despite this. Although, deep down, she must have known.

She smiled and waved goodbye.

It is the middle of the afternoon yet Wallace's car is parked in front of the house. Inge, coming from her aborted tea with Sheila, is made sick with fear at the sight of it. Forgetting the unpleasantness at Sheila's, she starts to run. When she reaches the front steps, she has to pause and grip the railing, a hand to her chest, panting.

"Wallace!" she calls from the door.

"Yo!"

He's in the kitchen spreading peanut butter on toast.

"What are you doing home?"

"I'm getting a cold."

"A cold!" She stares at him. "Don't eat that! No! I'll make soup."

"Mom."

"Run a bath. Now. Go." She points a trembling finger.

He puts an arm around her shoulder, leans his head against hers. Their two skulls clunk. Wallace says, "Ow," and walks off rubbing the place.

"As hot as you can stand!"

Bouillon cubes. She's filled with shame. There's no time to go to the store for fresh chicken. She chops the onion on the board, weeping tears of gratitude—to whom?

He's safe, for now.

An hour later, she carries down a tray. Still bath-pinkened, Wallace lies under the yellow field of flowers with his hands behind his head, twisted tissue plugs in both nostrils. He sits up when she comes in, arranges the pillows to lean against.

"Take those things out of your nose." She sets the tray across his lap and sits on the edge of the bed, anxiously watching his first sip. "It's no good," she says.

"Delicious!"

"Really? It's only bouillon."

"Needs salt."

She speaks slowly, not meeting his eye, looking at the age-speckled hands in her lap. "Wallace. You are not going to believe this. I'm out of salt."

"I took it, Mom. I'm sorry. I meant to pick up another box."

It occurs to Inge to feign surprise. Now she can ask. A whole box? What would you need a whole box of salt for? Instead she says, "Do you remember those girls? When you were little, they came and took you and Lisa to their Saturday-Sunday school."

"The haunted house?" He sucks broth off the spoon.

"Is that what it was?"

"They blindfolded us and made us put our fingers in bowls of stuff."

Inge recoils. "What stuff?"

"Peeled grapes. They said it was eyeballs. They poked sticks into our backs and said it was the Devil's horns. Lis loved it. She told them our dad was dead. We had a seance."

"You had nightmares."

"I was scared shitless."

She thinks how to phrase it. Why is there a knife in a box of salt under the bed, Wallace? What kind of meetings are you going to, Wallace?

"How's your case going?" she asks.

"Which one?"

"The fellow who's never paid taxes."

Wallace lowers his spoon in disgust. "He's against taxes. He's not against roads, of course, or doctors, or parks, or the sewage system. These he's enjoyed for twenty-three years. He's only against personally contributing to them."

"It's hard to believe people can be so selfish."

"Selfish?" says Wallace. "He's more than that."

She places a hand on her child's forehead. He looks up at her, still her child.

"What?"

"Nothing," she says.

"It's just a cold."

"You finish that and get some sleep."

"Stop worrying."

That next Saturday morning when the doorbell rang, Inge told Lisa and Wallace to stay where they were at the table. She opened the door to the dark-haired girl with the bunny barrettes, chin skinned, one knee stained red with Mercurochrome. She must have had a fall. In the middle of her smile, she flinched with pain and Inge felt a spasm of pity for her.

"Lisa and Wallace aren't coming anymore."

All week, Wallace's backward glance had haunted her. Haunted her until she placed it. Old photographs. Children being loaded onto trains.

"I don't know what you're doing," Inge went on, "but it's not nice to frighten little children."

"It's just a game."

"Does your mother know?"

Back in the kitchen, five-year-old Wallace gazed at her with grateful eyes. Lisa scooped swollen Shreddies out of her bowl then let them plunge back in the milk, over and over. All day long she punished Inge with her sulking.

Why then, Inge wonders climbing the stairs, why is Wallace attracted to these dark things? Pentagrams and knives. She shakes her head. But what is he actually up to? Sacrificing babies? Hanging

crucifixes upside down? A man who thinks not paying taxes is—
what? Evil? He works for the Crown! No. Whatever he's up to,
it can't be that bad.

She reaches the top of the stairs absolved.

Later, she sits down to a bowl of unsalted soup herself, has
barely taken a sip when the doorbell rings. Wearily, she refolds
her napkin.

Sheila is on the porch waving a brown envelope. Inge is annoyed to see her again so soon, to see her here at all. But the
woman has cancer, Inge remembers, and she swallows the wasp
of her resentment.

"How are you feeling?" Sheila asks.

"Better, thank you."

"I found it!" she sings, flapping the envelope again.

"I'm sorry. Found what?"

"Those damn papers I need a witness for."

Inge steps aside. "Come into the kitchen."

Sheila peeks in every door they pass and clucks. "Very nice
home. Are these antiques?"

"I suppose. It's my mother's furniture."

Inge doesn't offer a seat. She wipes the kitchen counter with a
tea towel to make sure it's dry. "I'll just get my glasses."

When she returns, Sheila has two documents laid out side by
side, open where the coloured tape is stuck on. "It's my will."

"Ah," says Inge, going over to the phone to get a pen. "Where
should I sign?"

"I have to do it first." Sheila *plicks* the pen from Inge's hand and
makes a show of putting on her glasses. "Watch me." She produces
an illegible flourish, then another. "I was going to write her out,
but I thought of something better. I'm leaving her a dollar."

Inge is taken aback. She's more than surprised. She's shocked.
Shocked that a mother could do such a thing, that she, Inge, would
be asked to bear witness to it. A shudder moves through her,

small but perceptible, and her right eyelid twitches. An electrical disturbance. What comes to mind is the image of the girl again, turning and running down Inge's front steps. A child. A harmless little girl. Who would guess? Inge watched her run down the steps and into the future. Three and a half decades would pass before Inge thought of her again.

Sheila is old and sick. In her mind's eye Inge sees her not as she stands before her now, triumphant with her avenging pen, but asleep on her feet at Aquafit in the chest-deep water. Sheila drenched and struggling out of the pool, clutching the railing, makeup smeared. Her scalp as pink as the inside of a shell.

# Hauska Tutustua

*Dear Mr. Elton,*

*We have received your letter dated 5 May, 2003, concerning the heir to the deceased Mr. Mikko Virtanen. All the information you provided to us we forwarded to the Ministry for Foreign Affairs in Finland. We will contact you as soon as we have a response.*

*Sincerely,*

*Sari Nurmi, Assistant to the Ambassador*

It was indeed hard to find. David counted—correctly it turned out, but for a quarter of an hour he wasn't sure—to the third un-marked gravel road. He set the odometer and measured the way from there. Some of the country he passed was marshy, probably Reserve, some forest. At 3.8 kilometres he slowed, watching the left side as instructed until he noticed a place where the lower boughs had been cut away to form a darkened arch. Shaggy tree arms scraped the roof of the car and for the few hundred metres that the driveway carried on David felt he was in a dream, or the victim of enchantment, steering over two red tracks spongy from centuries of fallen cedar. At last a clearing opened at the end, large enough for a mobile home, the shed behind it he hoped wasn't an outhouse, a pit to burn garbage, and a silver New Yorker put to rest under cedar boughs cut and laid across its hood and trunk and roof.

He climbed the wooden steps and knocked. Beside the door, over a decomposing cardboard box of serious empties, hung a flower basket filled with yellowed stalks.

"What?" Weak, from inside.

"Mr. Virtanen? It's David Elton from the Hospice Society. Did they tell you I was coming?"

He filled the long pause wondering what he would do if Mr. Virtanen died during the visit. This replaced his previous fear that Mr. Virtanen would already be dead by the time he found the place.

"I can't get up," Mr. Virtanen finally called out. "They took me to Victoria yesterday. I had the radiation."

"Can I come in?"

"I don't care. Why not?"

David opened the door on a great stink, like the trailer had farted. He covered his nose and came inside, followed Mr. Virtanen's coughing and found him in bed, a huge moustached man with yellowed hair and yellowed whites around the fierce blue of his eyes. He looked entirely tobacco stained and certainly his fingers were. David shook his hand and introduced himself again then went to empty the Mason jar that sat on the bedside table even though they'd told him Hospice volunteers weren't required to perform domestic duties. He wasn't going to sit and chat next to a jar of cloudy-looking pee.

"Don't you have a homemaker? I'll open a window. Do you mind?"

"She couldn't find the place."

"I'd be happy to drive her out. Can I get you anything?"

"Jesus Christ. I'd love a tea."

He hunted for the teabags in every cupboard in the kitchen, even under the sink where there were at least twenty pickled herring jars of striated fat, before noticing the tin on the stove. "What do you take?" he called.

Mr. Virtanen coughed up the word sugar.

David helped Mr. Virtanen sit up in the bed and rearranged the pillows. The cases, stained almost to transparency, reminded him of bacon grease on a paper towel. He placed the cup carefully in Mr. Virtanen's hands, held the sugar bowl up. "Tell me when." He had to break through the crust. "Just nod," he said after four spoons. Mr. Virtanen nodded at six.

"So Mr. Virtanen."

"Mike."

"Mike. I know a little bit about you. You were born in Finland, is that right?"

The Hospice Society had given David a file with general information about his client and suggestions for facilitating conversation. He'd been a logger, but now Mr. Virtanen could hardly raise a mug to his lips. *Find something you have in common.* Other than the obvious, David and Mr. Virtanen were both widowers. That was it. Most traces of Mrs. Virtanen had vanished. A dirty sham on one of the pillows. The bedspread was pink but Mr. Virtanen had covered it with a grey wool blanket. David still kept things exactly the way Marilyn had.

Mr. Virtanen slurped tea through the filter of his moustache. He closed his eyes and sighed a word David didn't quite hear. *Swami,* it sounded like.

*Bring pictures of your family. Be prepared to talk about yourself and your interests to start things off.* David had left the envelope containing the photos in the back seat of the car. Slipping out to get them would only give Mr. Virtanen another chance to die.

The huge hand slackened, leaving the cup of hot liquid balanced in the folds of the blanket.

"Is the tea all right?" David asked.

Snoring replaced the coughing and David took the cup away. He looked around the room while he waited for Mr. Virtanen to wake. A giant's steel-toed boot sat on the dresser beside a coffee can filled with shells. Hummocks of dirty clothes all over the floor. He glanced at his watch and decided: ten more minutes. He'd leave a note. He hoped Mr. Virtanen could read.

As soon as David stepped out of the trailer, he inhaled a great draft of air to flush his lungs. His chest burned. He was able to manoeuvre the car backward through the trees, but once on the road he began to cough. He opened the windows, but the cold air only made the coughing worse. It got so bad he had to pull over. Now he was dizzy. His every breath seemed to be drawn from a sticky wet bag inside him. Should he turn on the flashers? Honk for help?

He rested his forehead against the wheel, trying not to panic.

David's sister, Susan, called that night. Since Marilyn had died, Susan called every Sunday from her Monday morning in Sydney, Australia, after getting the kids off to school. David and his sister had ended up on opposite sides of the world. The dark of his night was Susan's eye-blinking noon, his winter her summer, but now, to his alarm, spring was nudging its way in. He had noticed the swell in the rhododendron buds, and crocuses—purple, yellow, white—colonizing the lawn.

"Do you have a cold?" she asked.

"It's just a tickle in the throat."

He was still in bed where he'd retreated after the careful drive home. He'd slept all afternoon and now it was dark. The phone and his own coughing had woken him.

"It's almost a year," Susan reminded him.

"Is it?" It felt longer. Much.

"Have you done anything, David?"

"What do you mean?"

"Have you cleared out the closets, for example? That would be a start."

She dropped the subject and moved on to her incidental news. Then they said goodbye for the week. Because he respected his sister, after their conversation he got out of bed and took a trial walk to the window. In the void of the Strait of Georgia, too overcast for stars, a barge was making its way up the coast, dragging its light. He was still coughing, but the vertigo was gone.

He went to the closet and randomly selected a hanger from Marilyn's side, a pale blue skirt and blouse she'd had made out of the silk someone had sent her. Who? She hadn't had a chance to wear the outfit. The Normans. After Bob retired, the Normans had bought a sailboat. Peggy had sent the fabric from Thailand. They'd missed the funeral. David remembered Marilyn unfolding the silk on the dining-room table, exclaiming. He paused to cough, then returned the outfit to the closet and took down the long denim skirt Marilyn had Saturdayed in. She must have hung it back up unwashed; it had retained the shape of her body. They'd lived together through many of Marilyn's sizes, David as constant at fourteen as eight.

As for his side of the closet, David saw that he was the owner of five identical white dress shirts and six in different shades of blue. He broke off coughing. Suits that he hadn't worn since the eighties found sanctuary here. He took three of the white shirts and four blue and laid them on the bed. He was ruthless with the suits, keeping one and the two tweed jackets they'd bought in Ireland. How many belts does a man require? He coughed again. When he'd finished with the closet, he started on the drawers, and by the time he went to bed he'd filled four garbage bags with his clothes.

The next morning he felt himself again, more or less, except for the irritating cough, so there was no need to call in sick. He put the bags of clothes in the trunk of the car to drop off at the men's shelter on his way home from work.

The second time he visited Mr. Virtanen, David was surprised by the improvement in the old man. In less than a week Mr. Virtanen was able to answer the door trailing forbidden clouds of smoke. The radiation had exhausted him, David realized. The same thing had happened to Marilyn.

"Out and about, Mike?" he said, sincerely delighted because he really, really did not want to stay inside the fuggy trailer. It was the cause of his breathing difficulties the week before, he was sure. "Do you feel well enough to go for a drive?"

Mr. Virtanen looked past David on the step. "What's that? A Honda?"

"It's made by Honda. It's an Acura."

One hand on the wall, Mr. Virtanen stepped on the back of his slipper and drove the other foot inside. When both slippers were on, he reached for David's arm and David helped him down the steps. They paused at the bottom where, like a weather vane reading a shifting breeze, the old man shuffled slowly around. He pointed to the shed. "That's my sauna." He pronounced it *sou-na* and David remembered he was a Finn.

"When did you come to Canada?" he asked when he'd got Mr. Virtanen in the car.

"Nineteen fifty-one," said Mr. Virtanen, sounding disgusted because, though David had moved the seat all the way back, his knees still kissed the dash.

"I was born in 1951," said David. "It might help if you recline the seat. There's a lever. A lot of Finns settled around here."

"I don't know any of them," said Mr. Virtanen, fumbling for the lever.

David started the car so he could open the windows and blow the smell out. Abruptly the seat released, throwing Mr. Virtanen flat on his back. "Jesus Christ!" he roared. He started to laugh. Then he started to cough. David got out of the car and hurried around to open the passenger door. When he was upright again, Mr. Virtanen hawked on the ground. It was, not surprisingly, yellow.

As soon as they got on the road Mr. Virtanen said he wanted to go into town. David nodded. A few silent minutes passed while Mr. Virtanen searched his pockets. The manila envelope of photos was still on the back seat. He should have given it to Mr. Virtanen so they could talk about the pictures as they drove. Mr. Virtanen took out a cigarette. No: a tight roll of bills girdled with an elastic band. "I like to go to the liquor store."

Relieved he wouldn't have to ask him not to smoke, David said, "Sure," and Mr. Virtanen magically started talking.

"I don't like these Jap cars. Too small. Only Japs can drive them. And the Japs get the jobs. No, I don't hang around with the Finns. If I wanted to be with the Finns I stay in Finland. Next time we go out in the New Yorker."

"You've never gone back to Finland?"

"No! I couldn't. I run away. I got a girl pregnant. I guess I ruined her life but she saved mine because I got away. There's no justice, eh?" He looked sidelong at David. "You're probably sitting there thinking cancer is my justice."

"I certainly am not."

"You're not religious?"

"No."

"I thought you were. A pastor or something."

"My wife passed away last year. A Hospice volunteer met with me. The volunteers visit the bereaved as well as the dying. I'm just returning the favour."

"What do you do with yourself?"

"Good question. My wife was the social convenor, so to speak."

"I mean work."

"Oh. I have an engineering firm. Elton Consulting. We do mostly infrastructure. Roads."

"Well. Cancer is because I smoke all my life. It's not justice. It's cause and affect."

When they got to the liquor store, Mr. Virtanen gave David his tube of money. "I only got my slippers on. You go in. Get a two-six of Finlandia."

He woke gasping. Somehow the pillow had fallen over his face. He threw it off and sat up in the dark, sucking, sucking, trying to catch his breath. He couldn't draw. His mouth hung open, useless. Then, from deep in his chest, something ominous. A long, low rattle.

Outside in the vast bellows of the ocean, fluid surged, retreated.

"It could be asthma," Dr. Cowan told him. "Or it could be a panic attack. Have you ever had one?"

"No. People don't suddenly get asthma, do they?"

"Sure they do. How are you otherwise?"

"Fine."

"The anniversary of a loved one's passing is significant." She'd been Marilyn's doctor too. "Very often people ask for help."

"Now this may sound silly," said David. "Is cancer contagious?"

"How do you know it wasn't a panic attack if you've never had one?"

Dr. Cowan arranged for him to have some tests done at the hospital the next day. That evening the Hospice Society coordinator phoned to tell him Mr. Virtanen had been admitted to palliative care and would not be going back home.

"He looked so much better last time," said a surprised David, though this wasn't really true. He'd looked just as bad, but with energy. Before Marilyn died she'd had the same vital spurt, like she was squeezing the last bit of life out of the tube. It had confused David. Just as he thought she was recovering, she died. She died of ovarian cancer four months after taking her stomach ache to Dr. Cowan. Susan, who had three kids, said the same thing happened just before a woman had a baby. Unable to waddle to the corner store the day before, she'd suddenly leap up, clean the whole house and bake a cake.

At the hospital, he blew into a plastic tube attached to a machine. They X-rayed his chest. Afterward, he went upstairs to see Mr. Virtanen. Of course he recognized the nurses and they, him. They greeted him by name at Save-On Foods too, but that was different.

Mr. Virtanen was sleeping. He looked yellower lying on clean white sheets.

A nurse came in to take his vital signs. "Hi Mr. Elton." David blushed. She was one of the nurses Marilyn had tried to fix him up with at the end. A red-blonde ponytail and slightly overlapping front teeth. He put her at twenty-three. What a joke. "Stop," he'd told Marilyn. "Please stop with the fixing up."

"Are you a friend of Mike's, Mr. Elton?"

"I'm volunteering with the Hospice Society now."

"That's so cool," she said and David started to sweat because he couldn't be sure that Marilyn hadn't been trying to fix him up from the nurse's end too.

"Is Mike going to wake up?"

"Probably not," she said.


The first weekend in May, David took out a suitcase and packed it with most of his remaining clothes. As he was doing this, the doorbell rang. He thought it might be the paper boy; he'd left a note suspending delivery. Instead he found a tall woman with short grey hair: Wendy French, the Hospice Society coordinator, out of context. He'd met her only once, at the volunteer training session. After that, all of their dealings had been by phone.

"I'm sorry. I didn't recognize you, Wendy. Come in."

"What a beautiful home," she said.

They'd had it built in 1980, he explained, when they first moved to Campbell River. On the cliff side was a deck with steps down to the lower garden. The plants there were all native, because of the wind. Forty-two stairs down to the beach. The sheltered front of the house, which faced the road, was where Marilyn had planted her rhodos, the reason he was packing. He didn't tell Wendy this.

"Coffee? It's made."

He came back to the living room where he'd got Wendy settled and set the tray on the coffee table. He felt perfectly adept at this task. When he and Marilyn had had dinner parties, when they'd hosted the folksinging group, he made and distributed the tea and coffee. Afterward, he cleaned up.

"I've got some bad news," Wendy said, taking hers black. "Mr. Virtanen passed away last night."

David set down his cup and coughed into his hand. "Oh, dear," said Wendy after a minute of this. "I'll get you a drink of water." She found her way to the kitchen and came back with a glass. David drank and the coughing eventually let up.

"I always deliver the news in person the first time. Sometimes volunteers have more of a reaction than they think."

David picked up a napkin and while Wendy busied herself looking for something in her briefcase, he wiped the tears out of his eyes, some of which were from coughing. He was surprised by his reaction, and not. Surprised because he hardly knew Mr. Virtanen. Not surprised because, more than the cooking, he found feeling the most challenging aspect of widowhood. During his marriage, he had only been vaguely aware of how strictly apportioned his and Marilyn's roles were. Marilyn emoted. David banked. He was pretty certain that had he died first, Marilyn would have banked with aplomb, but he couldn't claim the reverse.

"Do you want another client?"

"Yes."

Wendy opened a file folder on the coffee table. "His name is Charles Wilson. He goes by Chucky. He's forty-four. A veteran. He's more or less homebound with HIV-AIDS."

David accepted the folder. He cleared his throat. "For the next few weeks I won't be at this telephone number in the evenings. You can still leave a message, or call me on the cell. Or at the Seaview."

"The Seaview Motel?"

"Yes," said David.

There were over thirty species of rhododendrons in the front yard, every possible colour, some taller than David, the smallest ankle height, all of them about to climax simultaneously.

*Dear Mr. Elton,*

*Enclosed please find a translation of the letter you received from Armi Kuusela. I actually didn't mind doing the translation at all. I was doing it at home, not on Embassy time, for practice. For your information, your correspondent has the same name as the Finnish contestant who won the very first Miss Universe pageant in 1952. You will find this and similar interesting facts about Finland on our website, www.factsaboutfinland.com. This month's feature article is about our annual World Wife-Carrying Championship!*

*Sincerely best wishes,*

*Sari Nurmi, Assistant to the Ambassador*

On Monday the hospital phoned David at work. He thought it was about his tests.

"No. This is with regards to Mr. Mikko Virtanen. You were his Hospice volunteer I understand."

"That's correct."

"Did he mention to you his final wishes?"

"Yes. He wanted a bottle of vodka."

"I mean his remains. Did he say what he wanted done with them?"

"It never came up."

"We're asking you because he has no next of kin and we need a signature."

"For what?"

"To cremate."

"He has a next of kin."

"He does?"

"He told me—well, there's probably a grown child in Finland."

"All right. That's not what it says here, but anyway. Mr. Elton, could you please contact Mr. Virtanen's next of kin and have him advise us on this matter?"

"Me?" David said.

The VSO came through town that spring. Marilyn and David were subscribers to everything, holders of every kind of pass. David had promised to keep it all up. On his beloved wife's deathbed he'd told a lie.

"And who are you going to do these things with?" she'd asked.

"I'll do them alone."

He didn't. He didn't ski anymore. He didn't folksing. He didn't go to plays or concerts until he found the tickets, the last in the series, for an all-Sibelius concert.

He asked Chucky if he wanted to go. David played poker with Chucky once a week in his basement bachelor apartment where Chucky was dying of his tattoos. "It was a dirty needle," Chucky had been quick to explain. "Man, I was a tattoo tourist. Everyplace I went in the army I got one. I'm my own charm bracelet." He was shackled at the wrists with Celtic knots and chains of Sanskrit. The snout of the dragon he carried against his heart poked out of his snaggy terry cloth robe.

"The symphony?" Chucky laid down a flush and David groaned.

"It's Sibelius."

"Who?"

"You know, the great Finnish composer."

"Never heard of him, but what the hell. I'm not doing nothing else."

When the evening came, though, Chucky wasn't feeling well enough. "I got those runs again, man. I got the chills." David was already dressed. He'd come to pick Chucky up. The tickets were in his pocket. Chucky had cancelled, but he'd called David at home when David was still at the Seaview.

The only unfilled seat in the Tidemark Theatre was the one beside David. The music swirled around him, thick and light, aggregate flakes. Out of the white, a parade emerged, then vanished. A thousand white birds lifted off a frozen lake. David knew practically nothing about Finland. Maybe Chucky had been. He pictured a tattoo of snow, blurred and white.

Every single moment he was conscious of the empty seat.

The next night was Sunday so he retrieved his messages from home. One was from the doctor, left on Friday afternoon. "Your test results are back. Everything looks good. Maybe you'd like to come in so we can talk again about the panic attacks."

David erased the message. He wasn't having breathing difficulties anymore. It had been some kind of virus, he presumed. He was bothered more now by recurring bouts of diarrhea.

He phoned Susan back. "Where were you?" she asked.

"At a concert," he lied.

"A concert! That's wonderful!"

He heard a bird in the background and tried to picture his sister in her backyard halfway around the world. He hoped she didn't detect any difference in the ambience from which he spoke. "Actually, I'm out and about a lot now. I'm volunteering for the Hospice Society."

"Oh. And what does that entail?"

"At the moment, playing poker. I visited an old Finn a few times before he died. Now I've got Chucky."

Susan sighed. "That's nice, David, but you know what I thought? I thought you'd gone out on a date."

Later he lay awake listening to the traffic on the wet highway, the muted laughter of his immediate neighbour's TV. Every twenty minutes the ice machine in the hall exhaled and released a clatter of fresh cubes. The parking lot was filled with pickup trucks, the motel with men. They were construction workers and loggers, men more like Mr. Virtanen and Chucky than David. David was the only one wearing a jacket in the morning when he ordered his takeout coffee and bran muffin in the restaurant. The others wore T-shirts, or plaid shirts, and caps. They tucked into steak and eggs, knives in their fists. Men's men. He admired how at ease they were in each other's company. If they needed any other kind, they picked up the phone and ordered her. David had heard this too, through the motel wall.

He got up to go to the bathroom again. Every time it embarrassed him to think of his sounds broadcast to his neighbour through the plumbing. Soon he could go back home. Tomorrow he'd pick up some Imodium.

Back in bed, shivering now, he pulled the stiff spread over himself. His teeth moved like castanets. The man in the next room had bought himself a movie. Groans and huffing. David lay there sweating, trying to ignore the affront of the soundtrack.

*Baby, do it to me! Your cock is so-o big!*

Christ, he thought.

*Harder! Harder!*

Clack-clack-clack-clack-clack-clack-clack went the ice.

In the middle of his tossing, his irritation, he realized what the matter was. Not asthma. Not panic attacks. Not HIV. He liked and respected women. Women's ways, their company. He could barely live without it.

Marilyn had been right.

Day by day he was dying of the lack.

"Now she's a nice-looking girl," Marilyn had said after the nurse had come and gone. "She speaks French, bakes bread. She grew up on Hornby Island. Her mother was a Québécoise hippie. She said she was twelve before she actually had a real pair of shoes on her feet. Her mother made sandals."

"Did she soften the leather with her teeth?"

"I think she's lovely. She's single, can you believe it?"

David asked, "What would you have done if I'd had an affair?"

"I would have chopped you into bits."

"Then why are you doing this?"

"There are a couple of things I want to make sure get done. Don't let loyalty get in the way of your happiness, David."

"I find this all very painful. You're obviously getting better."

"The rhodos? They need deadheading."

It wasn't only David. She had a penchant for matchmaking. When a newcomer appeared on the scene it wasn't long before Marilyn had ascertained his status and issued a strategic invitation, though her only successful match was Joanie Highcroft and Martin Abel. Marilyn had invited Joanie to one of their monthly folksinging Thursdays so that she could meet the new engineer in David's office. The new engineer contributed a bottle of Scotch to the potluck and proceeded to drink most of it himself. "'Stairway to Heaven' is not actually a folk song," Marilyn tried to tell him. Joanie left early with a headache. She staggered down the driveway cupping the sides of her head. Martin, their non-singing next door neighbour, was putting out his garbage and he offered her Tylenol. "Imagine what I go through every month," he said, inviting her inside. They sort of knew each other anyway—it wasn't that big a town.

Marilyn, later: "Timing. Timing is everything. You see, Martin's divorced now."

Late in May, David went back home. Some of the rhodos were still flashing their joie de vivre, but most had grown weary of the party. Next year, he thought. Next year I'll be able to look at them.

In the pile of junk mail inside the door was a reply from the Finnish embassy in Ottawa. He read it and, even before he had unpacked, duly phoned the hospital.

"What a coincidence," said the clerk, the one with the clipped dry manner he'd talked to before. "I was just going to call you."

"Why is that?"

"We have limited room here, Mr. Elton. Perhaps I didn't explain that."

"Sorry?"

"The freezer's full."

"Well, I heard back," said David. "He's got a daughter."

"What did she say?"

"They've located her. I've got her name and address."

"But Mr. Elton," said the exasperated clerk, "I understood you were going to write her."

*Dear Ms. Kuusela, you don't know me, but . . . This letter may come as a shock to you, Ms. Kuusela. Ms. Kuusela, I'm writing you on behalf of the . . .* It took him several days to get the wording right.

The reply came four weeks later. A single transparent page of Bic'd Finnish he couldn't read. The very words were epic, some of the letters, the *U*s and *M*s and *N*s, as indistinguishable as one wave from another.

Amazingly he found both a Finnish-English Dictionary and *Teach Yourself Finnish* at the library. He stood between the shelves flipping pages.

*Hauska Tutustua.* Pleased to meet you.

"David?"

When he turned, a woman seized him. "David! It's so good to see you!"

Evidently he was acquainted with his embracer. Who was she? Peggy! Peggy Norman, from folksinging. He stiffened with shock. The last time he'd seen Peggy she and Marilyn were on the couch, leaning into each other, heads touching, harmonies spilling out. They were the only decent singers in the group. All last year Peggy and Bob had been away sailing around the world. They'd sent Marilyn a river of blue silk.

Peggy released him. "I'm sorry, David. I'm so sorry."

He glanced down at the glossary so he wouldn't have to meet her eye. *Errikoissaastohinta.* Special economy fare.

"We miss you at folksinging."

"Marilyn especially, I'm sure."

"Bob left you a message a few weeks ago. Did you get it?"

Peggy had come back. She'd gone away and she'd returned. Here she was, squeezing his arm. Oh God, David thought. Marilyn wasn't. She really wasn't.

"Won't you join us again? Even just once? I know it won't be the same."

He put his free hand in his pocket, felt the thin envelope. "I'm volunteering for the Hospice Society now."

*Tulevaisuudensuunnitelma.* Future plan.

"That must keep you busy. It's a good cause."

"Yes it is." David touched the smooth skin of the letter. "They have nobody."

Dear Mr. Elton,

First excuse me for writing in Finnish. I speak a little English but my writing leaves something to desire. I was very surprised receiving your letter. Naturally I knew I had a father but my mother was a bitter woman and she refused to speak about him. When I saw the envelope I was thinking, who do I know in Canada?

How good of you for taking the trouble to contact me! I hope you will not mind doing me one more favour. I will be coming on 3 August in order to arrange my father's affairs. I am flying to Victoria and will be taking a bus to Campbell River from there.

Mr. Elton, I would really like to meet you, if you would be so kind.

Gratefully,

Armi Kuusela

# Ring Ring

Hello? Hello Peeps. Mama it's Peeps, Harrison tells her. Are you coming for Christmas, Peeps? Mama he's coming for Christmas!

Christ—days and days of cold rain, cold wind, cold—mas. A delicious frisson moves through her. She's poaching on the sheet in bra and panties, spread-eagle so no part of her touches herself.

Okay, bye Peeps.

Harrison replaces the cordless in its cradle, climbs onto the bed, on top of her, and lies with his heavy rank head on her chest. Almost unbearable, the hot press of his body. The live toad of his heart pulses between them. This close would kill a toad, yet it's she who's dying—of heat and waiting, of boredom, of playing telephone in a hot room.

Ring ring. He lifts his head to look at the phone. Clambers off. Hello? Hello Sam. Mama it's Sam! When are you coming over? Now? Mama Sam's coming over!

If I took a shower. If the phone really rang while I was taking a shower.

He wants to talk to you Mama. It's Sam.

He waggles the receiver in her face. Heat has her pinned to the bed. She can barely lift her arm. Hello Sam. I'm expecting a call. Could you phone back? She hands him the phone. Here Harrison, he says he'll call you later.

Her bathrobe has slipped from the plastic Ikea chair onto the floor in a faint. She sits on the edge of the bed staring at it. The mere thought of fabric touching her skin. It'll be hotter on the balcony with the sun lasering down on the back of the building, on the glutted Dumpster in the alley, its contents turning to juice.

Two drags, she thinks. Two drags or I'll go crazy.

Harrison has replaced the receiver again. He takes two dirty fingers, inserts one in each nostril. Grubs.

Dumpster stench, fried chicken stench. She flicks the lighter, dully expecting the unmoving air to ignite. A moustache of perspiration sprouts as she sucks the hot smoke in. Below, Roto-Rooter slowly trolls the alley, crunching over diamonds. The balconies of the facing buildings expose themselves: bicycles, junked furniture, mops, buckets, toys, coolers, bleach bottles, mattresses, dead plants in plastic pots. Some are fringed with laundry. Rap music punches out.

Harrison steps onto the balcony in his underpants, bare feet on concrete. Ow! He hops back inside.

The phone rings. She fires the cigarette over the railing. Harrison, inside, has a head start. Don't you answer it! she shouts.

*Ring.* His hand hovers above it, feeling the sound.

It's my birthday Harrison. Do you have a present for me?

Forgetting the phone, he dashes to the apple box in the living room where the toys live when they aren't all over the apartment. *Ring.* She takes the key off the nail, steps out into the hall. The door shuts behind her. She looks up and down, clutching the robe. The neighbours are mostly muffled voices anyway, and cooking odours. *Ring.*

Hello. She inflects it with boredom.

Bella Pizza.

Huh?

You a calling Bella Pizza.

Ha ha. You called me.

What for you laughing? Pepperoni? Anchovy?

I'll hang up.

You hang up. Plenty a people wanta my pizza.

Okay. Pepperoni. When should I pick it up?

I deliver.

Harrison calls from inside the apartment, Mama, Mama!

I'll pick it up. When'll it be ready?

Mama! He pounds on the locked door.

She's always ready.

She opens the door on Harrison holding out a tangled wad of toilet paper in two hands. Happy Birthday Mama.

Is this a present? She kneels on the carpet, probes the loose layers. Inside is a wooden block. Just what I always wanted. Do you feel like visiting Mrs. G?

Ring ring! He dashes off. Ring ring!

It's here.

He runs back and grabs the phone from her. Hello? Hello Mrs. G. Mama it's Mrs. G! She wants me to come over!

She has to call Mrs. G now. Every time she worries that Mrs. G will say no.

On the phone, Mrs. G thanks her profusely, as though she is the recipient of the favour.

When she gets out of the shower, Harrison is on his stomach, half swallowed by the futon couch, legs, thin and calicoed with bruises, sticking out.

What are you doing?

He squirms his way out, sits up cross-eyeing a finger. Too late, she sees the snag of light. He pops it in his mouth.

I told you not to eat that stuff!

Trees, stars, bells—glitter shapes unstuck from Christmas crafts buried in the carpet, resurfacing even now. Last time she vacuumed she put her hand to the nozzle and felt hot air blowing out.

Outside is so much cooler. She feels guilty for keeping Harrison inside all morning, all day yesterday and most of the day before. She combs her wet hair as they walk the two blocks to the little stucco house with the chain-link fence. There's a sign on the gate: *Pick Up Dog Refuse*. She and Harrison pass it on the way to the park and every time she puzzles over *Refuse*. If Mr. G is in the yard impaling garbage with a straightened hanger, or using a shovel to scoop shit off the verge, they go by without speaking. Mrs. G hollers to him in their language: Vincent-eee! If Mrs. G is outside she insists on running in for a treat for Harrison. Once she invited both of them in for something special she baked herself. Harrison shook his head. It's dirty. It was poppyseed cake. Mrs. G laughed and laughed. Another day she said she'd be happy to have Harrison come over for a visit if his mother needed a break.

She's waiting for them at the gate. On a normal day Mrs. G wears loose cotton dresses and weird elastic knee socks that squeeze the flesh of her legs over the top. When she's expecting Harrison she puts on a good dress with a belt, high heels and makeup, as though she has a date.

Harrison! She waves.

Without a backward glance, the child marches up the walk. Wave to Mama, says Mrs. G, pleased that he forgets her so easily. She waves too, then turns her back on the spectacle of the girl. Hair wet, black T-shirt with dirty bra straps showing. Spelled out in rhinestones: *It's Hard Being a Princess.* On her skinny bottom she wears a miniskirt of camouflage material. God help them should there be another war.

Wincenty, having watched the unsentimental parting from a slit in the drapes, opens the door wearing the face he puts on when he discovers a pit in his cherry soup. A ring in her nose! What is she? A pig?

Harrison knows to take his shoes off. He struggles.

Baba will help.

No! The naked foot pops out of the too-small runner, almost throwing him off balance. He looks at her in surprise, then laughs the giddy head-thrown-back laugh of a drunk.

He goes directly to her bedroom, to her closet, where he drops to his knees before the altar of the shoe rack. As though on stilts, he rises unsteadily onto the gold pumps, taking her hand for balance.

Clop, clop, clop to the bathroom. She wipes the dirt off his face and hands with a damp cloth. Clop, clop, clop back. He perches on the padded stool before the mirror and selects a jar. She tells him what it's for. Wrinkles. He opens the lid, inserts a finger, draws it down one cheek, then the other. Satisfied, he picks out a perfume. Oh, this is my favourite too. Her hand over his, she helps him spray his wrists. He notices her nail polish.

First I trim your nails. Do a proper manicure.

She fetches a sheet of stationery from the desk in the hall, cuts his nails so the tiny dun crescents land on the paper. Carefully, she folds it into a square and tucks it away in the drawer.

He wants pink polish.

Clear is the best for little boys. See? So shiny.

Hands spread open on the table, he blows with her.

Are you hungry?

I want a necklace.

Of course. She sets the box before him, letting him unlatch and open it. He likes the amber beads best and looks at her to tell him again what's trapped inside. This is pollen. You know, dust from flowers. Here's your little friend, Mr. Spider. Do you like cherries? I have cherries.

How does Mr. Spider get out?

He's in the bead forever, but he's happy.

Why?

Because you're looking at him.

Ring ring.

Oh my goodness, says Mrs. G. There's the phone.

The lopsided rotation of the KFC bucket is something she's taken for granted all her life, like the movement of the earth around the sun, but now it's still. From where she stands at the bus stop, she can see the girl behind the counter, not statue stiff, wound down like the bucket, but paging through a magazine.

The bus pulls up with a derisive hiss. She boards clutching her Baggie of change. The driver doesn't look at her for the three stops it takes her to feed pennies into the fare box. Then someone else gets on and he waves her back. I need a transfer, she says. You have to pay the correct fare to get a transfer. He presses a lever and all her coins clatter down. Asshole, she mouths.

Here, says a Native man, handing her his transfer as she passes.

Oh cool. Thanks.

She moves to the very back because she doesn't want to sit with him. East Broadway sliding by, she squeezes handfuls of her hair so it won't dry flat. Her thighs stick to the seat and every time the bus stops, her skin feels like it's ripping off.

A woman gets on with a lot of shopping. A song plays in her purse. She takes out a phone. Hello? I'm on the bus.

A girl with ponytails and a Ouija board gets on. She says to the

Native man, I don't think it works in a moving vehicle.

She'd *so* love a cellphone. This is what she's thinking when her dream comes back.

At Alma she gets off and waits for the Number 10.

He opens the door and starts right up the stairs, leaving her standing there.

Could I get a drink of water?

Help yourself, princess.

She really is thirsty, but she also loves the house. It's so cool. She's been twice before and this time she goes through the living room to get to the kitchen. There's a genuine fur rug that she stands on in her bare feet for a second. One wall is filled with a picture, a grey background with a black circle that looks like it was done with a paint roller. She can't say exactly why she likes the picture, but it makes her feel like painting isn't that hard. She feels inside the circle. The other wall is a window: dollops of mountain, silver water.

The kitchen tiles are cold. She takes a glass from the cupboard. They don't even have ordinary drinking glasses but heavy thick-sided ones that make water look like greenish pop.

She goes up the carpeted stairs. He's lying on his bed in shorts and a T-shirt. *Cat—the other white meat.* It kills her to think he's been lying for three days in exactly the same position as her, not phoning.

She goes over to his bookshelf. What did you dream last night?

What?

Do you remember your dreams?

Sometimes. I dreamed once I won the Nobel Prize. I went to collect it and they wouldn't let me in the building.

She finds the book, exactly where it was last time, fans the pages to *N*. It's here. If you dreamed of winning this prestiggious prize—

Prestigious.

—you are being cautioned against arrogance and reminded of what goes before a fall—

He lifts his arm off his face. What *is* that?

*The Dreamer's Dictionary.*

Did you bring it?

No. It's on your shelf. Tell me another.

Look up fellatio.

What?

No. Orgy.

How do you spell it?

D-U-H.

Really.

O-R-G-Y.

Orchids. Organ. Orgy. This dream is a warning that your excesses or repressions could get you into trouble.

Oh please. Repressions.

I dreamed last night that I was at this, like, incredible party. It was outside, in a garden. She finds the *P*s. Everyone was dressed up and there were waiters and everything. It was, like, so cool.

He sits up, plucks the book out of her hand and, before she can stop him, stuffs it down the side of the bed. She stares at him.

Get it. Go on.

He'll slap her ass. She knows he will. She's not stupid.

There's nothing more boring than listening to someone else's dreams.

She looks away, hurt. Takes out lip gloss, daubs her bottom lip. He shoves her down on the bed. When she screams, he claps a hand over her mouth.

Shut up. We've got neighbours, dummy.

He straddles her, pinning her arms under his knees. His nostrils are two completely different shapes, she sees now, one round, the other a teardrop. You don't notice head-on. He twists the lip gloss out of her hand.

Don't, she says as he digs a finger in the pot. She thrashes her head, but it's useless. He runs a line down her nose and cheeks, dots her forehead one, two, three.

Mrs. G and Harrison lie together on the bed, Harrison sucking on the beads. Lulled by the ticking fan, his thickened breaths, she slips into a dream. Harrison stands at the end of a long line of children. You, someone says. And you and you and you and you and you. He is going down the line. Her little sister is gone, but he hasn't yet reached Harrison when the telephone wakes her.

Wincenty answers in the kitchen. Stupid. The only person who would phone in the middle of the day is a telemarketer.

Water drips off his penis. He went to the bathroom and washed her off. She's hurt until she sees he's holding something out to her. She sits up. It's a wad of toilet paper. Oh, she says. That's so sweet.

He means for her to wipe her belly with it.

What's that? he asks, pointing at the purple leech above her pubic hair. Get your appendix out?

She wonders about him then. He might actually be younger than she is. This is his parents' house. She's figured that out. Don't you do anything? she asks.

Oh thank you very much. What do you call what I just did?

I mean work.

Work!

She smiles. She so likes how he talks. He doesn't say he's unemployed. He says he's *unemployable*.

Under the heap of clothes on the floor, a trill. He squats and finds his shorts, takes a cellphone from the pocket, flips it open and turns his back, tucking the hand not holding the phone into his armpit. Hello? There's a small hollow above his buttocks she's never noticed. That makes two more things she knows about him.

Nothing, he says. Nothing.

She squeezes past. She wants to wash the lip gloss off her face. Nothing.

When Harrison wakes, she takes him to the kitchen where Wincenty is eating cherries.

Take the pits out for him.

No, says Wincenty.

She gives the boy his milk and sits down herself. See this tool? Do you know what it's for? He shakes his head. Watch. She inserts a cherry, depresses the plunger with her thumb. Pop! Out comes the pit!

The boy laughs.

She puts the hollowed cherry on a saucer for him. Wincenty eats it. No!

You pit them for him, you pit them for me.

Fine. Two little boys, one an old man. She pulls his plate closer and pits one for Wincenty, one for Harrison.

Afterward she gets up from the table to wash her hands and dump the pits into the garbage. The boy sits with a clown-mouth stain on his frown, staring at Wincenty.

Why are you doing that?

What did he say? Wincenty asks.

He's asking why you're doing that.

What?

Doing what, Harrison? What is Wincenty doing?

Opening and closing his eyes.

I'm blinking! Wincenty roars.

Then the doorbell rings and Mrs. G's heart falls to the floor.

When the thought crossed her mind, she invested some hope in the girl not ever coming back.

The old man answers and looks her up and down. He's disgusting, she thinks. He walks with a cane. He probably can't even get it up any more, so why does he bother?

Harrison reeks of perfume when he hugs her. The old lady wears too much and it rubs off. Thank you, she tells Mrs. G, who comes after him with a face cloth.

Harrison. Let me wipe your face.

I really appreciate it.

Not at all. Any time. She gives up with the cloth and waves. Bye Harrison! Bye for now!

Harrison pushes out the door without acknowledging the farewell. She squeezes the back of his neck until he stiffens. Say thank you to Mrs. G.

Shrinking down, he mouths it to her feet.

It's too hot to fight. She waves to Mrs. G as she leads him away by the hand. When they are through the wire gate, Harrison breaks free and runs.

It must have been a Christmas or a New Year's party. She was having the time of her life. A waiter offered her a drink off a tray and a good-looking man put a cigarette in her mouth. Everyone was good-looking and so was she, she assumed, or she wouldn't have been invited. *A dream about a party is a good news/bad news symbol of mixed fortunes and contrary omens.* So true! she thinks. One of the other guests asked her a question she couldn't hear. Yes, she answered. A son. *Oh my God!* she thought in the dream. *I have a son! Where is he?* She spent the rest of the party in a panic looking for him.

She feels sick just thinking about it and stops to light a cigarette. Harrison has run ahead to the corner. He's looking right at her, purpled mouth and chin, waiting for her to catch up.

Mama?

His expression is so sombre, for a second she thinks he's about to hold her accountable for what happens in her nightmares. What? she asks. What do you want?

Am I wearing underpants?

The apartment feels even hotter now that they've escaped it for a while. She plugs in the kettle to make him a Mr. Noodle while Harrison, on the kitchen floor, pries the magnetic numbers off the fridge and lines them up along his arm. She fills the Styrofoam cup halfway with boiling water and when the contents have softened, tops it with cold from the tap.

Here. She sets it on the table.

Meow.

Here's your supper.

Meow. I'm a cat.

She puts the cup on the floor. He gets on all fours and lifts the dripping ringlets out with his mouth.

She goes to the living room where it's cooler and lies on the couch. On the ceiling, the smoke detector pants, open-mouthed. Black wire tongue, red wire tongue. Heat. Boredom. Waiting.

Waiting.

Waiting.

Harrison, bibbed with soup, comes into the living room. Bun-bun and Paddington are on the floor. Harrison uncouples them and brings her Bun-bun.

Hello, he says in Paddington's voice. Hello? Hello? Hello!

Hello, squeaks a weary Bun-bun.

How are you today?

Fine, she says.

I'm not talking to *you*! I'm talking to Bun-bun!

The phone rings. She lunges off the couch though a second earlier she couldn't imagine ever rising from it again. Don't you answer that! Time out if you even *touch* it! Time out for *the rest of your life!*

It's the old woman. It's Mrs. G saying, There's something I forgot to tell you. He went to the toilet while he was here and, oh my goodness, produced an enormous portion.

What she doesn't tell the girl. What she keeps for herself. Bending over to wipe him, she glanced into the bowl.

A gold star riding on it.

She straightened with a gasp, disbelieving her own eyes.

Miracles, every time he comes.

Wincenty is still grumbling when she gets off the phone. A tattoo!

And you, he says. You act like you're in love.

Ring ring, says Harrison. Ring ring.

# *Spleenless*

During the last days of the supposed millennium Manfred had a dream. A knife. His furry abdomen. The keen point dimpling the flesh, a secondary umbilicus. He watched in horror as the blade, in two violent bloodless pulls, ripped past his pelvic bone, turned sharply (how else?) at his right hip, then carved along his rib cage and around until the jagged circumnavigation of his bowels was complete. Viscera tumbled out and Manfred woke up screaming. Curled and panting on the sheets, wet with sweat, obliterated by pain, he was no longer himself. He was his pain.

Eventually his thoughts returned from wherever they had scattered, but with each new wave fled again. Each time, a flotsam of memories. His lurid, teenage obsession with gore. (Strangled with his own intestines? *Neat!*) His Aztec approach to the female heart in later life. Shame redoubled the next agonizing wave, bringing with it Omi, his long-dead granny. Omi and the wiry pad she wore tucked into her hair at the nape. At night it slept in a saucer alongside the German Bible. These were her instruments of terror: *Herr Rat* and Lutheran excess. Now, at long last, little Manfred was being punished, and justly, for all the hurt he had inflicted in his life. His pain now was the pain he had caused and the pain he had tittered over, boomeranging back.

He thought of a wild animal crawling into the underbrush to die privately, with dignity. If someone had to be there, it should be the person you really love. Yet here was Susan, panicking in his ear. "Manfred? What's wrong? Answer me Manfred."

Manfred croaked, "Call Annelie."

"I'm calling 911!"

Hell, Omi had said, would be different for each person. For Manfred it turned out to be an eternal middle of the night on a stretcher in a busy hospital corridor, his supplicating groans ignored. Susan made entreaties on his behalf, but they seemed to be backfiring. "He's dying! Dying!" Well, why else would he be here? They'd met four months ago in a Yaletown gallery. Overhearing her effuse over his particle separator series, he'd sidled right up to her flattery. Nothing as insightful had passed her lips since.

Susan squatted beside the stretcher. "Honey, I'm trying to get you something for the pain."

Her night breath made him writhe. Attuned to the oceanic rhythm of his agony, the changing tides of his throes, Manfred braced for another swell. He was going to die in the arms of a woman he didn't find interesting.

"Please," he mouthed. "My address book. In my desk. Annelie."

"I'm not leaving you, Manfred. What's her last name? I'll use the phone book."

"Stadel."

"Stadel? Who is she? Your sister?"

Shiny white room. Masked faces staring down. Voices far away, deep with reverb. No more pain. Blackness slowly covered him. Feet, knees, thighs. The parts it passed over turned to liquid. Abdomen, chest. Death: a darkroom. He had regrets. And what about his photographs? What would happen to them?

He woke in sunshine to his very idea of a nurse opening the blue curtain around his bed. Cool fingers played with his pulse. Alive! "In all my fantasies," said a groggy, elated Manfred, "this is where I pull you down on top of me."

"In your fantasies you probably have a spleen." She handed him a plastic cylinder attached to a cord, like the control on a slide projector, a black button on the end. "This is your morphine. Push here when you need relief."

"You trust me to do this?"

"Manfred! You're awake."

Susan came unsmilingly over and collapsed in the chair by his bed. He tried to push himself up, grimaced and pushed the morphine button instead. "What did we have," he asked, "a boy or a girl?"

Her eyes were swagged in dark hammocks of fatigue. Everything else on her normally colourful face had blanched. She spent an hour in the bathroom every morning, carried an extension cord in her makeup kit so she could sit in comfort on the edge of the tub while she blow-dried her hair upside down. Now her hair, dyed rust, looked like it needed a good watering.

"I wish you'd told me you were married, Manfred."

"I'm not married."

"You were. I'd think you might have mentioned it."

"Who's the tattle-tale?"

"Your ex-wife. You got me to phone her, remember?"

He remembered now and quickly changed the subject. "Check this out, Sue." He lifted the sheet. "I've been fitted with a catheter. This is the life."

A Japanese man in a suit came in, made straight for Manfred's bed and shook his hand.

"Can I help you?" Manfred asked.

"I'm Dr. Ito, your surgeon. How are you feeling, Mr. Stadel?"

"I feel fantastic."

"That's great." He gestured to Manfred's nether regions. "May I?"

"How do I know you're a doctor?"

The man produced a stethoscope from his suit pocket.

"How easy is that to come by?"

Chuckling, Ito unsheeted him. He untaped the rectangular dressing that covered the incision and, after a cursory glance and three painful kneads of Manfred's abdomen, repackaged him.

"Imposter," said Manfred.

"We're supposed to leave for Mexico the day after tomorrow," Susan told the doctor. "We're going to see in the new millennium on a Yucatán beach."

"It's not actually the millennium," said Manfred. "She won't listen."

"I hope you have cancellation insurance."

"Do I get to take it home in a bottle?"

"You don't want to. It wasn't pretty."

After the doctor left, Susan got out of the chair and bent to kiss Manfred. "I'm going home to get some sleep, honey. It's been a long and terrible ordeal." She paused in the doorway and looked back. "Oh, Manfred? You're welcome."

Manfred waved. He gave himself a few hits and fell cheerfully asleep, waking later to the ministrations of the nurse who looked even better after he'd topped himself up.

"Are you going to be the one who takes out my catheter?"

He fell asleep again and when he woke, didn't feel so good. It wasn't the pain. After his night in hell, the incision hardly ranked. Something was missing. Something had been taken from him. He felt a void greatly out of proportion to the space the pinkie-long sack of blood that had been his spleen would have taken up. Hollow and aching, clutching the morphine dispenser in his fist, he abandoned himself to the meagre consolation of self-pity.

A different, older nurse came in and offered him a suppository. "How kind," Manfred sniffed. She turned a crank at the head of the bed, raising him painlessly to a sitting position. Then dinner arrived on wheels under a dull steel dome. Manfred had done his share of food shoots. A monochrome meal won't taste good because it doesn't please the eye.

Meat in gravy, whole wheat bread, chocolate pudding.

On Manfred's left the curtain made a partition. In the facing bed an elderly man, dappled with age spots and eager to talk, reached for his dental plate. It was soaking in a water glass on the bedside table beside a can of Poppycock. "Prostate?"

"Pardon me?"

"Are you here for your prostate?"

"Spleen."

"Where is that anyway?"

Manfred pointed vaguely.

"These other fellas are both in for their prostate." He pointed his chin at the curtains that gave their roommates privacy—from him, Manfred guessed. "I came in with some bad stomach pain but it turned out to be an impacted stool. I'm pretty tickled. For a few hours there it looked like I wasn't going to make it to the next millennium."

"You might not," said Manfred. "It's next year."

The old man tucked into his own brownish dinner while Manfred only eyed his. Eventually a lank young man appeared in the doorway, interrupting the standoff.

"Manfred?"

At first Manfred didn't recognize the visitor. He hadn't seen Michel for several years, not since Annelie's wedding when Manfred, this time a guest not the groom, had gotten drunk and made a cautionary speech. His pale successor hadn't made much of an impression at the time except that Manfred distinctly remembered hair.

"Michel. You shaved your head."

Michel petted his crown.

"Come in." Manfred pointed to the baby strapped to his chest. "What's that?"

"This is Clara. Now don't give me that, Manfred. Annelie sent you an announcement."

"It's yours?"

Michel nodded. Father and daughter were equally hairless with identical close-set blue eyes. They might have been conjoined twins, attached at the heart, back to front, one of them hideously stunted.

Manfred pushed his tray aside. "Is Annelie coming?"

"She's getting the lowdown from the nurses. How are you feeling?"

Wounded, he wanted to say, but to Annelie. "Check this out." Manfred showed him how the morphine was self-dispensed. "Push here. Go ahead."

Michel pushed, his eye on the light above Manfred's bed.

"Ah!" Manfred sighed.

The baby grabbed the device and stuffed it in her mouth. When Michel pried it away and gave it back to Manfred, she began to cry. Pockets were searched, a pacifier inserted. The baby spat it out on the bed. Michel tried a rhythmic bending at the knees. The baby flailed her limbs like she was doing jumping jacks.

What's a baby for? Manfred asked himself.

Then his muse arrived, his apple-cheeked child bride, and Manfred felt the knife again, this time in his heart. Gone were the tangled teenage tresses his fingers used to catch in. With short hair Annelie looked even more like Lee Miller. Lee Miller's head superimposed on the much plumper body of Kiki of Montparnasse. She'd put on weight. "Fat and happy" came to mind. When she'd been married to Manfred, he'd made her so miserable he could lift her with one hand. Yet she brightened when she saw him and opened her arms. He wasn't mistaken. She crossed the room, her face aglow with love.

Michel released the fussing baby from the harness and passed the hot potato on. Annelie started nuzzling, practically licking the baby.

Quick! Another hit! Manfred scrabbled for the cord. Michel's baby was Annelie's too? How had he missed that?

"Well, Manfred," she said. "You're human after all."

On the ward everyone was making resolutions. His roommate Mel vowed to eat more roughage over the next thousand years. "Go on, Manfred. There must be something about you that needs improving."

Manfred told him, "I accept myself exactly as I am."

Later that afternoon they kicked Manfred out. "I'm not weaned yet," he protested as they drew the IV from his hand. "Would you tear a three-day-old baby from the breast?"

"Dr. Ito will set you up with a nice big bottle of Tylenol 3," said his favourite nurse, Diane, originally from Fort McMurray, youngest of three daughters, age twenty-four, size eight dress *and* shoe. Her resolution for the coming millennium: to leave those split ends alone!

"There's no one to look after me. What if I relapse?"

"What about that woman who was here?"

"She's in Mexico."

A male nurse with a tattoo took out the catheter. A cab was called.

All day Manfred lay in the bed of his own unmaking, as he liked to refer to it. Getting up hurt, but eventually he had to do it. In the bathroom he peeled back the dressing then nearly swooned at the sight of the incision in the mirror, a crimson path through the dark forest of his belly hair. From solar plexus to navel he was tacked together by black thread. Why so big a cut? He shuffled to the kitchen and made himself some tomato soup, then, still on red, ate the rest of his mother's bird's nest cookies shipped from Mississauga, licking the raspberry jam out of her thumbprint. He badly wanted to phone his mother and tell her what had happened, but she would insist on flying out and nursing him back to health and after three days of her he'd start bringing up the usual scarring childhood incidents just to make her cry.

He went out onto the balcony and looked down on Yaletown. His neighbours had stripped their Christmas trees and were maypoling the light posts with tinsel. Vancouver City Council, for once showing moral initiative, had declined to put on a party of any kind and now these deluded citizens were taking the festivities into their own hands. At the Starbucks on the corner, groups of laughing patrons gesticulated through the steam of eggnog lattes. A man on the corner, "homeless" according to his sign though nevertheless in possession of a dog and a guitar, busked "Auld Lang Syne." Fools! Manfred wanted to shout down.

Back inside, he steeled himself and lay down on the couch. What had they taken out? Absurdly, what came to mind was Man Ray's first Dadaist work, *Le Cadeau*, a flatiron with fourteen tacks glued to its underside. Then everything he had ever misplaced: keys, unprocessed rolls of film, scraps of paper scrawled with urgent messages, the very core that made him Manfred—a purple-faced, stump-limbed manikin, his darker self. Here he lay, a husk of the man he had been, the bran of him, needy and sentimental. Next he would be taking pictures of sunsets and kittens.

In portrait photography, everything depends on the sitter's expression. He could not erase from his mind the picture of Annelie at the hospital, the look of love he'd coveted, then, over the subsequent days, appropriated. Her cooing surely included him.

By eleven the revelry in the street below, though an hour short of climax, threatened to bust his seam. Manfred dressed and called a cab.

Blocks before they reached the Burrard Street Bridge, he saw the giant illuminated *2000* held aloft by a construction crane. "It's not really the millennium," he told the turbaned cabbie. "One, two, three, four, five, six, seven, eight, nine, ten. So—1991, '92, '93, '94, '95, '96, '97, '98, '99, 2000. Get it?"

They passed Kits Beach where a party was going on. He heard music, the salvo of firecrackers. "Another thing. How long are we going to have to say *Year* 2000? We didn't say *Year* 1999. I've never claimed to be born in *Year* 1952. It's madness. Are we going to be expected to say *Year* 2001 too?"

Annelie's house in Point Grey stood in darkness. The entire street seemed to be asleep, the house-poor and the double-mortgaged peaceful in dreams of debtlessness. With no response to his first tentative knock, he tried again, louder. Then the porch light came on and in his blindness he waved away the cab.

Annelie opened the door and blinked over the chain. He remembered writing dirty limericks all over her naked body. *There was a young woman from Punt* ... What happened to the negatives?

"Manfred!" She popped out the clear horseshoe of her mouthguard and wiped her lips with the back of her hand. "Thank God. Do you have an emergency kit in your car?"

"Why?"

"I couldn't get any candles. I went over to London Drugs around five but they were sold out."

"What do you need candles for?"

"When the electricity goes out."

"Anneliebchen," he said. "Midnight has come and gone in St. John's. In Winnipeg. In Cranbrook."

She hovered there, not quite believing him. "My computer's going to be all right then?" She unchained the door and in tartan pyjamas, squinty and uncombed, stepped aside to let him in. "What are you doing here, Manfred?"

"I wanted to see you."

"Now? If you only knew how long it's been since I've had a decent night's sleep."

Left standing on the mat holding his gift, he watched her climb the stairs. Manfred faced facts: the back view of her was hardly the pride of Scotland.

"Michel," he heard her say. "Wake up. Manfred's here."

Collusive whispers.

"I don't know," said Annelie. Then, "That won't work. He always does exactly the opposite of what you ask him."

Michel slept in the nude, Manfred observed as his rival descended the stairs cinching the belt of his robe. From this vantage, Manfred could see up the robe almost to where the real competition dangled. When Michel reached the bottom of the stairs, the two men stood nose to collarbone. Unlike Manfred and Annelie, Annelie and Michel were not a physical match but victims of a comical disparity in height. They were a lot closer in age, however, and Manfred suddenly felt like a mean old uncle dragging the children out of bed.

Michel checked to see if his stubble was in place, then pumped Manfred's hand. "Happy New Year, Manfred."

Manfred gave the gift to Annelie along with his coat.

"Michel, Manfred says my computer's going to be all right."

Michel had gone ahead to the living room to turn on a light. "I told you that."

They followed. A complex stereo system filled most of the shelves. Lit with so many coloured lights, it reminded Manfred of the Doomsday machine. Michel dragged a plastic flying-saucer-like baby seat closer to the armchair and put his bare feet up on it, crossing one long white leg over the other and flipping the robe to cover his naked thigh. Manfred sat beside Annelie on the couch. He breathed in sharply and extracted a plastic pretzel from underneath him. "That's a hell of a subwoofer you've got there," he told Michel.

"So, Manfred. What's this you've brought us?" Annelie tested the weight of the gift with both hands.

"It's a present for the baby."

She tore away the newsprint Manfred had wrapped the book in. "Ah, Man Ray. Look, Michel, it's a book of Man Ray's photographs."

"Let me see," said Michel.

"Man Ray is Manfred's idol."

"I wanted to be Man Ray," said Manfred.

"He wanted to be Man Fred. Remember how Manfred wore a shoelace instead of a tie to our wedding? That was because Man Ray always did."

"Well, after about 1941," Manfred corrected.

Michel sat back down with the book. "Schöenberg had a little affectation I've always wanted to take up." He turned a few pages. "Manfred! We're putting this away until she's eighteen."

Outside: cheering, kazooing, the clash of pot lids. Michel leapt to his feet and disappeared down the hall. "Oh, God," Annelie groaned. "Is it midnight already?" She rose with a yawn and headed to the front door where she slipped on a pair of oversized shoes. Manfred followed, struggling off the couch then stepping sock-footed into the chill night nailed down with stars. The street light on the corner wore a halo. Alone. The moment to speak was now.

"Anneliebchen."

*Clang clang clang! Clang clang clang!*

"I hope this won't wake up Clara." She pressed her lips to Manfred's cheek, the cold tip of her nose qualifying their warmth. "Happy New Year, Manfred."

"You've kept my name all this time, Annelie. Why?"

She stifled another yawn. "It would have been confusing at work if I changed back. No one would know who my memos were from."

"I've been thinking."

Her eyes widened. "Don't do that!"

"I remember once, you got out of bed in the middle of the night—"

"Manfred? No. We are not going to have this talk. We've been on friendly terms all these years."

"I moved over to your side and pressed my face to the pillow. It was wet with tears."

"I drool, Manfred. Because of the mouthguard. You've had a scare. You've felt your own mortality. That's what this is about."

"I'm sorry for how I treated you."

"Well, I'm happy to hear you say that. Better late than never. But what about that poor woman who phoned me at four o'clock in the morning? How are you treating her?"

Michel stepped out onto the porch wearing headphones. A tape recorder that could easily have fit into Manfred's abdominal cavity hung by a strap over his shoulder as he threatened the sky with a huge, phallic microphone. Manfred drew Annelie to the far corner of the porch, almost tripping over the stroller. He plainted her name.

"Shhh." She pointed to Michel and, finger to her lips, clomped back inside.

Manfred obeyed, keeping quiet until the last nasal blats of distant noisemakers died away. Michel kept on listening, but to what? The ambient sound of the universe, the low hum of electrical infrastructure, the ceaseless grating of tectonic plates? At last pushing the headphones over the back of his head so they ringed his stalky neck like a horseshoe, he gave the nod.

Back in the living room, Manfred eased himself down on the couch while Michel rewound the tape. He pressed Play. Hearing the feeble cheers again, Manfred said, "Y2K. What a farce."

His own voice on the tape, tremulous with love: *Annelie.*

"Midnight snack?" Michel asked. He took his gear with him.

He was a sound composer, Manfred remembered, then couldn't help but hear what came from the kitchen a minute later as a prosaic symphony: cupboards opening, cans meeting the counter, Cellophane crackling, something like cereal pouring out, fridge seal breaking, drawers tried. The electric can opener revved a crescendo and out of nowhere a grey cat appeared and shot a startled green look at the supine Manfred. Meowing, the oven door yawning and slamming, water running. The microwave's SOS, bottle caps pried off.

"Ta da!" Michel carried in a platter and, with a foot, manoeuvred the flying saucer seat over to the couch to set it on. Tortilla chips fused with hot cheese, piled with refried beans, black olives, avocado, salsa, sour cream—an abortion of colour.

Manfred forced himself to sit up. "Ow, ow, ow."

Michel returned a second time with his equipment and two bottles of beer. He joined Manfred on the couch where they listened to midnight for the third time.

*Annelie.* The hollow tattoo of Michel's clown shoes taking her away.

"Where's Annelie?" Manfred asked.

"She probably went back to bed. Clara's teething. She's up a lot in the night."

Manfred heard the cupboard doors opening again, the cans connecting to the counter, the fiery crackle he knew now was a bag of tortilla chips.

Michel said, "We're listening to me making nachos while we're eating the nachos. Do you get it?"

Manfred stared at him. He had nothing against the boy really. His eyes were too close together, but other than that he actually had no feelings for him either way.

"It's about Time. Hey! Better idea!" He wiped his hands on the front of his robe, slipped the headphones back on and fiddled with the buttons. The microphone reared between his thighs. "Now I'm recording us eating the nachos."

"Can we talk?"

"Sure." He took off the headphones. "Of course we can. Shoot. How can I help, Manfred?"

"I mean do I have to be quiet?"

"No. I'll just edit you out."

Manfred, forced now to contribute his crunches to the service of Art, ate self-consciously. Salsa dribbled down the front of his shirt. He drank half the beer in one go.

"So how does it feel not to have a spleen?" Michel asked.

Manfred unbuttoned his shirt and peeled back the dressing.

Michel recoiled. "God! Should you be out of bed? Should you even be out of the hospital?" Down the hall something squawked. "There's Clara. I'll be right back."

Here was Manfred's opportunity to sneak upstairs, but his relationship to his pain had changed he realized then, the standard against which he'd first measured it, the actual rupturing, three days distant. He managed to get off the couch and as far as his coat hanging in the hall, and to feel through the pockets for the bottle. In flagrant disregard of the label, he shook three tablets into his palm. (Do they call it Tylenol 1? Do they call it Tylenol 2?)

Stairs? Out of the question.

He brought the Man Ray book over to the couch. When he saw the microphone balanced on the arm, the machine still running, he briefly slipped the headphones on. "Whoa there, Princess," Michel was saying over the baby's crabbing, as clearly as if they were in the living room. "Let's get you all changed up."

Manfred opened the book.

"Here we are, nice and fresh," Michel said, bringing in the lump. She gaped bluely at Manfred. "Another beer, Manfred?"

But when Michel returned from the kitchen, only the baby had a bottle. "Looks like we put away the last two. How do you take your Scotch?"

*Warning: May be habit forming. May cause drowsiness. Avoid alcoholic beverages.*

"Neat," said Manfred.

Michel poured the Scotch at the sideboard. Perched on his hip, the baby kept watch, taking the occasional pull on her bottle. Manfred could guess what she was thinking. He lifted the nude of Lee Miller to show her. She grimaced.

Michel handed Manfred his whiskey and returned to the armchair. They all drank, Clara on her father's lap. She reached for Michel's nose. "Beep," he said and she dropped the bottle and leaned into him with an open mouth.

"Ow!" Michel cupped his nose. "Someone has teeth." To Manfred: "It's a different life once you have a baby."

"Can I hold her?" Manfred asked.

Michel hesitated. "Just watch your scar there."

He brought her over and set her in Manfred's lap. Manfred was surprised by how warm she felt, how squirmy. "Aren't you a little package of life?"

She looked up at her father. "That's a good girl," Michel said.

Manfred tried with Man Ray again. "See here, young lady. Does this or does this not look exactly like your mother?"

Clara pulled the book to her and gummed it.

"She's hungry," Manfred said.

Michel offered the plastic pretzel off the floor then leaned down for a closer look at the book. When Clara took the pretzel, he whisked the book away and scrutinized Lee Miller.

"Maybe the eyebrows."

"The lips," said Manfred. "They've been seen floating in the sky."

Michel yawned. "Not lately."

The baby blinked up at Manfred and pressed a tacky palm against his cheek. It stuck there. "Ba ba ba." With Manfred's retort, "Ba ba ba to you!" she smiled, revealing four tiny blue-white teeth. How long had it been since he'd gotten such an unequivocal reaction from a female? He placed a hand on her head, cantaloupe-sized, velvet-fuzzed. Her neck was cowled in fat, chin non-existent, glazed with drool. These features notwithstanding, she was a beautiful blue-eyed thing. He saw it now and understood that the baby, not Michel, was his rival. Michel was nothing. And now Manfred wanted the baby. He glanced up at Michel still turning the pages of the book. How to get him to leave the room long enough to tuck the baby under his arm and escape? He would flee the country and raise her as his own daughter in Liechtenstein or Borneo. Like her mother before her, she would be his muse. His Kiki. His Lee Miller. His Juliet.

When he woke it was to a grey light erasing his dream, as though it had been floating in a tray of developing fluid. He was still in Annelie's living room land-mined with baby toys. Pain tightened her barbed arms around him. All the different-coloured eyes of the sound system had watched and knew more about the night than he did.

In the hall, he frisked his coat for the Tylenol.

Michel slept on his stomach, Manfred saw when he'd finally scaled the stairs and was standing in the bedroom door. Annelie had her back to him, covers mounded over her so only the side of her face showed. She made a formidable hump in the bed.

He lowered himself on one knee and drew the covers to her shoulder. The weight of her head squashed her cheek against the pillow, puckering her lips. "Anneliebchen," he whispered.

Her eyes flew open. She lifted herself onto an elbow and looked around. "Manfred? What are you still doing here? What time is it?"

"I used to love how the light caught on the fuzz on your cheeks."

"What?"

He took her hand. "The world is going crazy, Annelie. You heard it yourself last night. No one even knows what day it is. Come away with me. We can go anywhere you want. You don't have to worry about the baby. Michel is competent. Or, what the hell, let's bring her. I've changed. I have no spleen. You're the only woman I ever loved."

"I'm the only woman you ever married. Oh, Manfred. This is how you get away with all you do. You can be so sweet when you want to."

"Annelie."

She rolled over, showing him the tangled brown back of her head. "Go home, Manfred."

He waited. He gave her time to change her mind. Eventually a long, slow breath seeped out of her. His love deflating. Manfred got up cringing.

Was it always going to hurt this much?

Downstairs, he sat on the couch to put on his shoes and saw the tape recorder, repository and digitalizer of the night's secrets, there on the flying saucer. Manfred tried staring it down then gave up and rewound the tape as much as he thought he could stand.

*Man Ray said—this was at the end of his life. He was interviewed. Do you know the work of Man Ray?*

*A little. You brought the book.*

*What was I saying?*

*The interview.*

*That's right. He was asked what had satisfied him the most in his life. What did he say?*

*I don't know.*

*Did he say his art?*

*Did he?*

*No. No, he didn't. No.*

*Do I have to keep guessing?*

*Women.*

*Of course.*

*He said women.*

*I should have guessed.*

*What would you say?*

*Air brakes.*
*What?*
*Or when the fridge motor shuts off.*
Manfred pressed Stop.

New Year's Day. All across the city, the country, the continent, the world over at this very moment men were waking to their shame, nursing manifold wounds—hangovers, sprains, broken resolutions. Some had lasting retinal damage from the glitter ball, the Catherine wheel, the Roman candle. Ears rang on with midnight. Colds, herpes blisters, overdoses, rejection. They suffered. January 1, 2000, and Manfred was not alone except in this: that today was the first day of the last year of the old millennium.

He rewound the tape to the beginning and started recording again.

This year was a gift. Manfred felt lucky. On the porch, waiting for the taxi, he looked up and recognized the sky from *À l'heure de l'observatoire, les amoureux*, flocculent with cloud, minus the lips. Then the cab appeared at the end of the sleeping street and advanced toward him, the only coloured thing. He started slowly down the steps.

Inside the house, sleep would erase everything.

# Knives

## 1

How badly the audition goes correlates with how late Shauna comes home afterward and how many boutique bags hang off her slender arms by string handles. Todd has pointed out that most people spend money when they get the job, not the other way around, but this was received with a shriek and a hurling of the bags, so he keeps his logic to himself now. He doesn't want her to be unhappy. He thinks she's brilliant. Only last week they watched her in a rerun of a Canadian cop show bleeding in a crunched car. She delivered her one and only line, "Save my baby," so convincingly that Todd had wept even though he knew the baby was a sound effect in the back seat.

He glances at the kitchen clock and, shaking his head, pours a capful of vinegar down the drain. It reacts with the baking soda, erupting in a white froth that connects the decades: sandbox volcano, beginner's chemistry set, drain maintenance.

The kitchen floor is already dry, the whole condo shining, Todd standing on the dining-room table in his socks DustBusting the light fixture, when Shauna arrives. Looking down on her, he's elated not to see bracelets of bags. But why the quivering lip and where the perfect smile?

"How did it go?"

"You'll never guess who I saw."

"Did you get the part?"

"Yes."

"That's amazing!"

She wrings her hands—one of those gestures that throws Todd off every time. Is she truly distressed or does she just want him to think she is?

"Guess," she wails.

"You said I won't ever."

"Darcy Roach. From the Dunbar house. Remember?"

Does he remember? Todd has *scars*. "Where? At the audition?"

"On the street. I recognized him right away."

Easy for Todd to imagine this fateful meeting. He helps her rehearse scenes all the time. Shauna clipping beautifully along, berating herself, Darcy Roach intersecting her path, smiling a white slash. But Shauna and Todd are married now. Shouldn't that fact have exterminated Darcy Roach?

Todd's thoughts turn white and bubble over.

"I'm sure it was him," says Shauna. "It looked just like him. I think."

2

Danny moves out of the house on Dunbar Street in May to join a coffee-picking brigade in Nicaragua. This is 1984 when they're students at the University of British Columbia. *Adios,* Shauna thinks. Good riddance! Never has she been so cruelly treated in all her nineteen years. Now she's anxious for someone else to move in and displace her humiliation because, until then, Danny's empty room enshrines it.

She approaches Abby first. "Shouldn't we get another house-mate?"

A pneumatic sigh—the bus pulling into the stop directly in front of the house—but it could easily be coming from Abby who shrugs and shuffles off with her plate of toast and p.b. to read the Bible in her room. Incapable of lifting her feet, Abby moves from bedroom to kitchen to bathroom like a plastic table-hockey player negotiating the slots. Shauna has never met a person less engaged with life, and it disgusts her. "If we don't," she calls after Abby, "we'll have to divide the rent three ways instead of four."

"As long as it's a woman," says Todd when Shauna puts the same question to him.

"It should be a man. So it's equal—men and women." She writes the ad and posts it on the notice board at Stong's where she's bagging groceries for the summer. *Available immediately, bedroom in shared student house with three dynamic housemates. Close to transit, UBC . . .*

Todd was jealous of Danny. This is the reason he wants another woman, but Shauna isn't about to fill a harem for him.

Todd is the first to have contact. "Actually," he says on the phone, "we're looking for a woman."

"The ad I've got here in my hand says *man*."

The mallet of a shiver plays up Todd's spine. "That's funny."

That evening the voice on the phone comes to the house. Shauna volunteered to show him around but Todd, in his room marking lab reports for the class he TAs, joins the tour when he hears the flirty tone Shauna puts on at the door. An aspiring actress, Shauna can assume any character she wants. With Abby she's the cruel younger sister, with Todd the puppeteer. This is closer to who she was with Danny, but with an edge to it. "Living room." She sweeps a hand to take in their collegiate poverty: Sally Ann's old couch, rabbity-eared black-and-white TV, carpet a slug-yellow, dirt-flecked shag.

"Here's Todd."

She doesn't introduce him as her boyfriend! Todd's chest constricts. According to the chore sheet it's Shauna's turn to vacuum. Then and there he decides not to cover for her this month.

"I'll just go get Abby so you can meet her too."

After Shauna leaves the room, Todd turns to Darcy. "Hi."

Darcy glances through Todd. Darcys only see other Darcys. And Shaunas. Darcys have evolved retinas that make the breasts and genitals of Shaunas appear to glow bluely, like neon. Todds, however, can see Darcys and when they do, they usually swim to the other side of the tank. At the end of the summer, when the police ask for a description, Todd will be amazed by what the women say.

"Darcy," Darcy says now, and Todd shudders, the way he did on the phone. It sounds like Darcy is speaking from the very bottom of a deep, deep hole. Though he extends a hand, he's still looking beyond Todd, watching for Shauna to come back.

The handshake feels clammy to Todd, an eczema sufferer. He notices that the nasty cut across Darcy's index finger doesn't affect his manly clamp. Darcy's T-shirt is tight, too, enough to snug a pack of cigarettes against his bicep. "We're actually a non-smoking house," says Todd.

Shauna drags in Abby dressed in a frilly pyjama top and shorts, her white legs thick and doughy, one side of her face hideously scarred with pillow creases. "He smokes," Todd tells them.

"He can do that outside. What are you studying, Darcy?"

"I'm doing my MBA," Darcy says, using his gaze and Shauna's body to pull himself out of the hole. "But I started this job."

"What kind of job?"

"Sales. It's going to be hard to go back."

"I'm in Theatre," says Shauna with a curtsy.

Todd doesn't believe in the MBA. He doubts Darcy's name

ever even appeared on a high school diploma. "We're looking for a student," he says.

Darcy turns to Abby. "I had a girlfriend named Abigail. She broke my heart."

Abby stares at him like he's just stepped out of the dream Shauna woke her from.

"Who's at the door?" Shauna calls from her room.

"Sears," the man in coveralls tells Todd. He X's where Todd must sign, then returns with the clipboard to the truck parked in the bus stop. A second man gets out of the driver's side.

Shauna joins Todd at the door and the two of them watch, speechless, as the mattress in its protective plastic is carried up the walk. *Vince*, according to the appliqué on his coveralls, whips a pair of cloth booties from his pocket to slip over his shoes. Shauna still hasn't vacuumed. Staticky bits of dirt cling all over the cloth.

*Brad* puts on his booties. "Where to?"

"Upstairs," Shauna says. "The room on the left."

"Excuse me?" Todd calls after them. "You're parked in the bus stop?"

He can't believe his eyes when the two go back for a box spring.

That night Todd lies curled around Shauna, awake in the perfumery of her hair, thinking, defensively, how he likes to be lying close like this on his three-quarter futon. Abby has a futon too. Danny used to sleep on a bright blue Ensolite pad. Darcy's room is just across the hall from Shauna's and, though Shauna never sleeps there on her foamie, Todd worries about her proximity to a superior nest. Todd is personally acquainted with people who have nowhere to lay their heads but the couches at the Grad Centre. Someone under thirty owning a real bed? Just what is Darcy trying to prove?

*Thud.*

He sits up, listening. When he hears it again, he gets up and pulls on his shorts. Protecting Shauna is his first thought, that he'd like credit for it his second.

The sound is coming from the front of the house. He creeps down the unlit hall, grit prickling the soft soles of his feet. Whatever the time of night it's always dawn in the living room, the street light a substitute sun. He peeks out the sheers. A car is parked in the bus stop, trunk open, a man leaning inside. Darcy straightens with a box in his arms.

But it's only the eighteenth! thinks Todd.

Darcy comes up the walk and drops the box beside the others before going back to slam the trunk. Already sweating over the bus, Todd begins to sweat over Shauna waking up. Darcy hauls a duffle bag out of the back seat, throws it on the sidewalk, drags another from the front. All this is nightmarishly illuminated by the yellowy street light, amplified by the quiet of the night. An occasional car goes by. How long until the bus comes and what if it has to stop?

Darcy starts up the walk lugging both bags. The key violates the lock and Darcy steps inside and flicks on the hall light, exposing the furtive, bare-chested Todd. "Hey, Tom. Give me a hand with these boxes."

"Todd. You'll wake everyone up."

"It's not even midnight," says Darcy, thudding up the stairs.

Todd hops to it, because he'll do it quietly. The boxes are identical and unmarked and, though the size of the proverbial breadbox, they weigh the proverbial ton.

Upstairs, he finds Darcy lying long on the queen mattress, a pillow of arm muscles behind his head. "Thanks, Tom."

"Todd."

"Over there." Darcy points where Todd should set the box.

Todd carries up two more before he starts to feel used. "You're not supposed to move in until June first," he says.

"I'm just dropping off some stuff. Is there a phone jack in this room? I forgot to check."

"Your car's in the bus stop. You should move it."

"Are you by any chance a fag, Tom?"

Todd takes an affronted step back. "No! I'm not!"

Abby peels her cheek off *The Bondage of the Will*. The night before, she had been reading Luther. There are two kingdoms. In His, Satan rules by holding captive those not saved by the Spirit of Christ. And now Someone is in the kitchen opening and closing all the cupboards.

She actually likes living here when Shauna is at Stong's and Todd at UBC. Every morning she gets down on her knees and scrubs out the bathtub, fills it, then lolls there until the water cools. She takes a breath and slides under, though the same old Abby resurfaces each time. Afterward, she eats breakfast in her little piece of Creation: pear tree scabbed with lichen, foot-long grass, bindweed holding together the rotten fence. No one else sets foot off the deck except to get to the laundry room.

Today, Someone is in the kitchen. Deprived of her routine, she forgoes the bath and slips to and from the bathroom.

"Abby?"

Her reaction is seismic. The whole house trembles with His voice.

"Is there any coffee?"

"Um." The strength drains from her legs. She grips the door handle for support. "Todd has coffee. Check his cupboard." She's very careful not to look at Him this time.

"Which is that?"

She ducks her head, squeezes past and, in the kitchen, shows Him where Todd keeps his food. She opens Danny's old cupboard—trail mix, brown rice, Inka. "You can use this one. Just throw out what you don't want."

She's still in her pyjamas!

"Thanks, Abby," Darcy calls after her, causing the framed paint-by-number picture of the racehorse to tilt on its nail in the hall.

She eats last night's crusts off her plate. Also earlier crusts and the brown flesh left on the apple core. She shakes out the seeds and eats the cartilaginous inside of the core, washing it down with stale water. Just as she's getting back into bed, He knocks.

What she will tell the police: He was so beautiful, I felt like throwing up. Eye colour? they'll ask and she'll start to weep.

Darcy looks in. "What do you take?"

"What?"

"Milk? Sugar? Are you busy?"

"Kind of."

"Well, if you can spare five minutes, Abby, I'd like to show you something."

"Have you always shopped here?" Shauna asks because she can't remember seeing Darcy at Stong's before.

"This is where I saw the ad for the house." He smiles.

He had prominent canines, Shauna will tell them. His hair was dark blond. No. Light brown.

She puts the steak in a smaller bag before tucking it in with the produce. A frisson passes through her as she squeezes the cold meat. The Dunbar house is vegetarian. Danny, a vegan, insisted on it so the dishes would not become contaminated. Abby lives on apples and feces on toast. Todd is too cheap to buy meat. Periodically Shauna suffers cravings.

When she gets home from work Darcy is in the kitchen. When did he move in? the officer will ask. She won't know exactly. Technically the first of June, but they gave him the key in exchange for his cheque.

Shauna asks, "What's that?"

Handles jut from the block. On the counter beside it is a cutting board made from the same reddish wood.

"Pull up a chair," Darcy says.

One of the onions she bagged for him this morning waits on the board, stripped of its papery jacket. He draws a knife from the block, flashes both sides, scrapes his thumbprint across the blade. "Ooo, baby. This is seven and five-eighths inches of chef knife. Our Petit Chef. Recipient of the Cooking Club of the Americas' Member Tested and Recommended Gold Seal-of-Approval. The blade—it's stainless steel. The very highest chromium and carbon blend. Why? Let me tell you. To ensure both optimum corrosion resistance and—and!—a durable edge. Furthermore, Shauna, an extremely hard, thin coating of boron carbide gives it added protection."

A silver arc. His hand blurs. The crisp whack causes Shauna to start. It happens a second and a third time while she blinks through the sparks.

Darcy steps back from the onion. "Damn."

"Are you hurt?" She touches his shoulder, her first confirmation that he's real. His body is hard under her hand, and cold.

He's crying—vegetable tears.

Four perfect wedges tremble on the board.

We all must live in the kingdom of The Devil until the coming of the kingdom of God. More than any of them in the house, Abby understands this. Daily and steadfastly, the righteous must resist the allurements of the world and the whisperings of Satan. Evil wants us. It wants to rule us completely. Unlike those who freely do the bidding of The Devil, the righteous yearn for the other kingdom, the kingdom of truth and grace which will come to pass when we are ruled, not by sin, but only by Christ.

Darcy sits at her desk paging through her address book. She stands beside Him, close enough to get a noseful. It's a burnt smell, cigarettes and brimstone. She's never had a man in her room before, not even Todd.

"The most important part of the knife, Abby, is the blade. Who's this Reverend Aden—How do you say it?"

"Adenauer. I used to go to his church."

"Ours have the traditional high-gloss finish. Best time to call him?"

"Not on Sunday. Or Wednesday night."

He doesn't even write it down. He remembers everything, except the actual numbers, of course. Everyone who has warned her about Darcy, including Reverend Adenauer who periodically devotes an entire sermon to Him, has told her to expect Him to be whip smart.

"The wedge-lock handle ensures a non-slip grip. What's Wednesday night?"

"Bible study."

She lets Him take her address book after they've gone through it. He explains why He needs it. "When I call these people, I give your name. Because they know and trust you, they trust me. More importantly, they trust my product. You trust my product, don't you Abby?"

"Yes."

"Good. Your satisfaction means everything to me."

That night, Darcy calls her into the living room where He and Shauna are watching TV—not the black-and-white one that was put out in the alley, but the big box of colour Darcy moved in with. "Hey! We're watching *Three's Company*. Come on." Darcy has cable. He pats the place next to Him and smiles.

Abby would prefer not to sit beside Shauna, but she does, because this is where He asked her to sit. On either side of her Shauna and Darcy laugh at the program exactly where the unseen audience laughs. Abby doesn't get it. It's as if the program is in another language.

Out of the blue, Shauna grabs Abby's wrist and shakes it. "Will you stop doing that?"

Doing what? Abby wonders. What was she doing?

Abby stops in the kitchen doorway after *Three's Company*. Shauna smiles, very nearly caught in the act. She's just taken the last scoop of Abby's Skippy and scraped it into the garbage. Her hand is still in the fridge, replacing the empty jar. It's for Abby's own good. If she didn't lie in bed all day eating peanut butter, she wouldn't be so fat. Waddling up to Stong's is the only exercise she gets.

Abby sways from foot to foot, patting her bangs, probably trying to decide whether or not to be in the same room as Shauna again. Her blonde hair is frizzy. When the light is right, it's a wiry halo flaring round her impassive pudding face. Shauna sees the radiance now.

Abby turns and shuffles off.

The next morning Abby has to go to the store. With Abby out of the house, Shauna goes to her room, which is across from Todd's, with the bathroom in between. She opens the door and steals a glance around at the unmade futon on the floor, the desk piled high with books and dirty plates. In the corner is an unmarked cardboard box.

Shauna goes straight back to Todd's room. "Guess what. Abby bought knives."

He plucks the earplugs out. "What?"

"Abby bought knives from Darcy."

"Why? He left a set in the kitchen."

"Exactly," Shauna says.

Todd's room was a den when a real family lived in the house. He shivers and, turning in his chair, sees Darcy standing at the sliding glass door that leads to the deck. Darcy's trying to see in, hands bracketing his eyes, but because it's brighter outside, Todd isn't sure if Darcy knows he's there.

He can't believe it! Darcy tries the door! Outraged, Todd tears out his earplugs and leaps to open it. "What do you think you're doing?"

Darcy steps inside. "I just wanted to see your space." He picks up Todd's graduation picture, chudders a finger along the spines of Todd's books. "*Fish Locomotion?*"

"That's my thesis topic. Fin action in *Sebastes paucispinis*. Listen. Your cheque came back NSF this morning."

Darcy sits on Todd's futon and tests it with a failed bounce. "You've got the best room, Tom."

"My name is Todd."

Darcy points at the Vaseline on the bedside table. It takes a moment for Todd to decode the leer. "What? It's for my hands!"

"That's what I thought."

For the rest of the summer Todd will stew over this remark. He'll peer again and again inside the black hole of Darcy's laugh. If anything, it makes the skin on his hands flake faster.

"You better write another cheque," Todd says.

Todd is unsecretly pleased that the cheque bounced; he's smug. It means he was right about Darcy. Later, when Todd is stir-frying for himself and Shauna, Darcy comes to the kitchen with his cheque book. Todd tells him, "You can add on the five-dollar service charge."

"I was just about to offer to do that. How do you like the knives?"

"What?"

"The knives."

"They're fine."

"The majority of people don't know how to sharpen a knife. They don't want to know how. That's what I especially like about this product, Tom. These are ceramic-coated blades. They never need it."

"What?"

"Sharpening."

"I added your name to the chore sheet last week," Todd says. "We rotate chores monthly. Another thing, we have an informal system based on honour when communal supplies like toilet paper and dish detergent run out."

"See? Now that's a keen edge. But check this out." Darcy digs in the front pocket of his jeans, wriggles out a fistful of pennies and places one on the cutting board. He disarms Todd of the knife.

The flash, the lightning strike of the blade, blinds Todd momentarily.

Penny halves ricochet.

When did Abby choose The Devil's kingdom? Not the day she voted for Darcy as a housemate, but back in January when they phoned her about the vacancy at the School of Theology residence. She'd been waiting since September to move there, but now she said no. All that fall Danny and Shauna's noisy lovemaking had driven Todd and Abby out of the house for long rainy walks. Todd's room was under Danny's and he'd come and knock on Abby's door.

A knock. She starts awake. "What?" Croaky, sleep-clogged.

"It's Todd. Can we talk?"

Six months she's been waiting for an explanation, but now she finds she doesn't care. Todd opens the door. She draws her knees to her chest, staring straight ahead.

"What do you think of Darcy?" he asks the tangled top of her head.

Abby says nothing.

"I don't think it's working out," Todd goes on. "His first cheque bounced."

"The second won't."

"He's on the phone almost continually. Every night that TV of his is blaring. That's got to bother you."

Abby meets his eye. He dares make reference to her feelings? They held hands! When she went home for Christmas, Todd drove her to the airport and kissed her goodbye—*on the lips*! He called her in Saskatchewan twice, saying he missed their talks. "They're driving me crazy," he told her. "Earplugs," she advised.

He had intentions. He did! He said, "Let me be frank, Abby. As a scientist, I can't accept the Bible as a literal truth. But I could accept it on another level." She'd had no illusions about bringing him to Christ. She wanted a boyfriend so badly.

He clears his throat. "So you don't agree we should give him notice?"

"Does Shauna?"

Todd would have complained to Abby about Darcy's undone chores too, but as Shauna has yet to get around to hers that would be disloyal. Last night Todd swept the kitchen for Shauna and found *nine* penny halves. And now that he's seen the state of Abby's room, the true state of Abby, he can no longer avoid the cold clutch of guilt. In a skewed act of contrition, he gets out the vacuum and runs it over the entire downstairs, except for Abby's room. With a violent snapping and crackling, a month of dirt and dust and penny halves is sucked up, his own skin too, filling the vacuum bag to bursting.

He initials the chore sheet on Shauna's behalf, grabs his wallet and walks the four blocks up Dunbar to Stong's and Shauna in her forest green tunic. The open sides are secured by ties. *Stong's* it reads. He's still working up the nerve to ask her to bring it home.

Two packages of toilet paper, onions, carrots, green pepper, zucchini, a can of tomato sauce. The cashier rings it up. "Spaghetti tonight?" he says to Shauna, who puts it all in a bag. Her breasts are a gentle curve of green. The smock ends at the top of her slim thighs. He wants her to be naked under it. "Can I talk to you for a second?"

Shauna steps away from the checkout and covers *Stong's* with folded arms. "What?"

"I want to give Darcy notice."

"Why?"

"Are you serious? He's been here a month and has yet to do a chore. Here I am buying toilet paper again."

Shauna rolls her eyes.

"I don't trust him. He sells knives."

"You didn't like Danny either."

"Untrue! Maybe not at first, but after I got to know him I thought he was all right."

Danny was President of the UBC Anarchist Club, an oxymoron if Todd has ever heard one. He called Todd's attempts to organize the house "fascistic," but after he broke up with Shauna, Todd had a lot to thank him for.

"You should get to know Darcy," Shauna says.

"Have *you* gotten to know him?" Todd whimpers.

Shauna hopes Todd will be out when she gets home, but she knows she hopes in vain. He has no life apart from her and his precious fish.

"Shauna!" he calls the second she steps in the door.

She finds him on his knees in the bathroom fastening something to the wall with a screwdriver. Danny's poster, still taped above the toilet, asks if their bathroom is breeding Bolsheviks. Looking at it now, Shauna barely feels pricked.

Todd's handiwork: three toilet-paper holders labelled *Todd, Darcy, Abby*.

"What about me?" she asks.

"You're with me."

Shauna bolts upstairs. Across the hall the phone cord disappears under Darcy's door. She hears him talking. Boron carbide. Corrosion resistance. A thin hard coating. Though the words mean nothing to her, she feels an almost irresistible persuasion in his tone. "I vacuumed for you!" Todd calls up the stairs. She slams her door and collapses onto her foamie, the way she learned in Stage Techniques.

Danny didn't believe in deodorant, yet she preferred his BO to Todd's soapy smell. Darcy smells like a brush fire. He speaks in the low rumble of a gathering storm while Todd's voice peaks insecurely at the end of every sentence. Why is dirty sexier than clean? Bad sexier than good? Mean sexier than nice? She and Darcy have been watching TV together every night and if it weren't for the thumb-twiddling lump of Abby between them, who knows what might already have happened?

The next week Todd hands Shauna an envelope from Sears. "Look who it's addressed to. Who is Thomas Dickson?"

"They sent it to the wrong address."

"What a coincidence!"

"Maybe it's for one of the guys downstairs." Two silent Chinese post-docs rent the subterranean downstairs suite.

Todd snatches the envelope back. "The bed. The TV. Then this scheme with knives. Now we find out he has an alias!"

"Give it here," says Shauna, slipping on her sandals.

She clacks out the kitchen door and down the deck stairs to the basement entrance. It opens onto the mildewy laundry room they share with the post-docs, the air a potpourri of garlic, Tide and ginger. The one who answers Shauna's knock wears a dress shirt buttoned to a choke. He nearly falls back when he sees her. She has this effect on people, which is why she thinks film is the better medium for her.

"I'm Shauna from upstairs." She can tell he knows. He's probably been watching her all this time. Men do. She hands him the envelope. "I'm just wondering if this is yours."

No way is his name Dickson.

Perplexity lifts his glasses. He takes the envelope over to the window in the kitchen area. "No. Not mine."

"What about your friend?"

He comes back, shaking his head. "Sorry."

"Oh my God!"

Startled, he looks over his shoulder to see what is worthy of her gasp. Not the wok on the stove. The knife block on the counter.

That night Shauna comes into the living room where Darcy is warming up the set for *Dallas*. "My dad's birthday is next month," she says. "Will you take a cheque?"

"Cash, cheque, credit card, flesh. Let's go upstairs, Shauna."

Her whole body tingles when he says it.

This was Danny's room. It used to be that whenever she came across something of his, which was several times a day—he left for Nicaragua with only what would fit into a backpack—she would take that ride again: shock, hurt, despair, rage. Danny: a Method actor's motherlode.

All Darcy has for furniture is the bed, sheets slippery, oil black. There are no blankets. Doesn't he get cold? He opens a box and lays out the knives. "The inclusion of the cutting board is a limited-time offer, Shauna, so you're wise to purchase now." Afterward, while he packs the box back up, she writes the cheque. It's a lot of money, a big chunk of next semester's tuition, but she's always been a daddy's girl.

"Write your SIN on the back, Shauna."

She stares at him. "What?"

"Your social insurance number. Jot it on the back of the cheque if you don't mind." He pats the bed and Shauna sits, lowering her gaze. "I want to tell you something. Promise you won't laugh."

Not for a second does she believe he's sincere. It's as if they're running lines together. "I promise."

He caresses the cardboard box. "It may sound strange, but I feel a calling. I want to help. Sometimes I can't sleep thinking of all the people who have only ever owned a cheap dull knife."

Shauna thinks of Danny picking coffee so the Nicaraguans can take up arms and defend the revolution. She thinks of Abby praying on her knees. Even Todd claims that his research may one day have a practical application. All Shauna's aspirations are self-serving.

"If you know of any others I can help, all I need are phone numbers."

When he puts his hand on her arm, she seems to lose all feeling in it.

Being there with Darcy finally undoes Danny.

It may be that Shauna is cocooning her hygiene products in toilet paper before disposing of them, or that she's one of those people who uses a metre when four or five squares would suffice, but Todd doesn't really think it's any fault of Shauna's that he's at the end of his roll already while Darcy's is untouched. He's also troubled, deeply troubled, by the Sears bill lying unopened on the hall table for a week. It could be that Sears made a mistake, but Todd knows this isn't the case. He knows because Darcy is so obviously the criminal type. But if Darcy notices Todd has opened the bill the jig will be up, so Todd carefully steams it and uses one of Darcy's knives to pry the seal apart.

Among the long list of items purchased under the name of Thomas Dickson are a Simmons Beautyrest mattress and box spring and the Sony Trinitron. So whom do they have under their roof, Darcy Roach or Thomas Dickson? Or someone else?

He picks up the phone to call Sears. "I'm sure they are dull," says a woman's voice.

"You can have them sharpened if you want to go to that trouble and expense, but the knives I'd like to show you, Mrs. Adenauer, never need sharpening. You *deserve* optimum corrosion resistance, Mrs. Adenauer. You *deserve* a durable edge. I have your address. I could come over."

Every hair on Todd's body rises as he replaces the receiver.

Later that evening Todd leaves his door open while he studies. The women are with Darcy, drawn like dumb animals to the canned laughter and flashing lights. Though the sound of *The Cosby Show* makes concentrating difficult, he doesn't put in earplugs. He can't concentrate anyway so he closes his book and begins to peel tiny strips of skin off his hands, half enjoying the sting. Tiny beads of blood well up. He licks them off.

Darcy finally goes to the bathroom. Todd gets up from his desk and waits. "Thomas?" he calls as Darcy heads back to the living room. Darcy walks right past!

Todd unclenches his hands and sees the bloody mess he's made.

That night, a strange sound. Though softer and coming closer together, it reminds Todd of the thud he heard the night Darcy moved in. In the hall, he hears it as a rhythmic thumping coming from Abby's room. He pictures Abby beating her forehead against her desk, but it just goes on and on, Todd standing in the dark, listening, trying to figure it out, his heart racing to match the pace.

A different sound, a long inhuman groan.

"Abby," he whispers at her door. "It's me, Todd. Are you all right?" He thinks about asking her to go for a walk, but doubts she'd accept. It's three in the morning.

A tiny voice: "Yes."

The officer will take Todd aside and ask if he knew what was going on. Todd will feel like a louse.

The light wakes then blinds Shauna. She sits up blinking. "What are you doing?"

"My eczema's flared up."

The malady is less annoying to Shauna than his pronunciation of it. *EC-zema*. Also, his name ends in two *d*'s.

Todd scoops Vaseline out of the jar, smears his hands. He wriggles into the buttercup-coloured gloves, flexes fingers, shuts off the bedside lamp. "Sorry I woke you," he says, laying a cold rubber hand on her waist.

Shauna shrieks.

"Sorry!"

"I'm sleeping in my own bed!"

She grabs Todd's shirt off the floor by mistake—a good thing because she meets a satyr on the stairs. She's at the bottom, a hand on the banister, about to climb, when his form unmerges from the darkness. She can't see his face; her eyes haven't adjusted. He's a shadow cinching up his robe. Gasping, she tugs down the T-shirt hem to cover her pertinent parts.

"Going up?" Darcy asks.

He fills the stairwell as she passes. She teeters, grabs his arm and for a moment has no idea where she is. It's as though they're suspended together in an amoral void.

"What are you doing up?"

"What are you?"

Poised on the middle stairs, neither answers. He lets her by but, like smoke, follows closely. On the landing, he rubs against her. "Shauna. Let me tell you, I'm no Petit Chef." She can feel it for herself, hard against her back, seven and five-eighths inches, plus.

What stopped her? she will wonder later. How did she summon the self-control? She says good night and closes her door. Just as easily she could have crossed the Stygian hall.

Abby saved her. Rather, Shauna worrying what Abby would think. Abby is God's proxy. With her around there is an account. If Shauna succumbed that night, she would have known every man in the house in the Biblical sense—except the post-docs.

At breakfast the next morning Todd keeps his sulky gaze on her while he mashes a banana in his bowl. Shauna refuses to meet his eye. She has nothing to feel guilty about. To the contrary.

At last he speaks. "I can't find my wallet. Do you know where it is?"

Shauna says, "I think we should be allowed to kiss other people." She decided this as she tossed in the flames the night before.

His look as he rises from the table, his staggering retreat—the losing duellist. The phone starts to ring as the front door slams, so she can't go after him.

"Did you give my phone number to someone?"

In the background, the wails of Shauna's infant niece.

"Rosie?"

"Did you?"

"Why would you think that?"

"A guy phoned here and said so. I never buy anything over the phone. He started arguing with me, so I hung up. He called again. He called *seven times*. He said he was a friend of yours."

Darcy appears in the doorway and Shauna knows he heard what she said to Todd. She's stunned to see the whole door frame filled, the top of his head grazing the arch, shoulders pressing either side. Is it possible that he's grown?

"Rosie, I'm late for work. I've got to go. I'll call you later."

Darcy takes the phone and drops it in its cradle. He backs her against the counter. She doesn't even try to resist. She's the one responsible for this beast. "Shauna," he says, singeing her with his breath. "This is a limited-time offer."

The kiss cracks her head against the cupboard. A metallic tang fills her mouth in advance of his tongue. Member Tested and Recommended. A durable edge. She's gagging by the time he lets her go.

There's Abby, transfixed in the doorway. "Hey babe," Darcy says, wiping his mouth with the hairy back of his hand.

"Oh, Abby," says Shauna. "It's not what you think."

Abby about-faces.

Making the best of an embarrassing moment, Shauna leaves for Stong's. She works all morning, sweaty with apprehension, putting the things other people buy into bags. Her mouth feels like banana mash. Then she remembers her granny who lives alone and defenceless in a little house in East Van. She makes the panicked call on her lunch break.

"Gran, it's me."

"Who? Rosie?"

"Shauna."

"Shauna! What a surprise!"

"How are you, Gran?"

"I'm fine."

"Oh, good. I'm just phoning to check—"

"Shauna, darling, I really can't talk just this minute. There's a young man here showing me the most marvellous knives."

The power of The Devil is not as great as it appears to be, Abby remembers as she scrubs out the tub. If He had full power to rage as He pleased, no one would be left alive. There is still more good in the world than bad. Only a very small part is actually subjected to the power of The Devil. He is compelled, after all, to leave the fish in the sea, the birds in the air and men in their cities.

She rinses the blue wash of Comet off the tub's sides, stoppers the drain.

Yet He is capable of causing great disturbances. He brings

kingdoms into conflict with each other and throws provinces and households into confusion. She who submissively serves The Devil abets this end and will suffer much for it, especially, most especially, in her conscience. Shauna clearly doesn't know this.

As for Abby, she's changing sides.

Todd isn't in his room when Shauna gets home from work. He hasn't come back from UBC yet. Probably Shauna is panicking for no reason. Why be alarmed? She kissed Darcy. So what? But when she lifts the phone receiver, the dial tone chills her to the bone.

She goes upstairs and knocks on Darcy's door, opens it and sees the big bed stripped to the mattress and not a single cardboard box. She goes back downstairs to the living room where the TV used to be. He's gone! *Hallelujah,* she thinks.

In the kitchen the knife block stands on the counter, one slot empty.

Shauna tries the bathroom door and, finding it locked, quails. She remembers Abby this morning. It wasn't the first time Shauna has seen her pain. Is Abby in the bathroom with the Petit Chef? Shauna closes her eyes. She sees *through* the door to what she imagines all this has led to and, even in her horror, marvels at how considerate Abby is to keep it all contained in the tub. If Shauna had done this to herself, she'd have made an unholy mess, purely for effect. Shauna would do it naked. In her mind's eye Shauna sees Abby lying in the tub in her pyjamas, her face, drained of colour, the same white as the frills around her neck. All her colour is in the water.

The Dunbar house is old. There are still skeleton keys in some of the locks. Shauna opens Abby's door to get the key from inside and use it to unlock the bathroom. The cutting board and knife block sit on Abby's cluttered desk. The empty box is on the bed. Abby is filling it with books.

"Ah!" says Shauna. "What are you doing?"

"Packing. I'm going home."

"Because of Darcy?"

Abby lifts her face. What a look. Shauna will feel judged for the rest of her life.

"Who's in the bathroom?" she asks.

Of course Todd never expected his relationship with Shauna to last. Six months ago he answered her tap at his door, thinking it was Abby. Tearful, Shauna asked if they could talk. Todd let her in and closed the door, hoping Abby hadn't heard the knock.

Danny broke up with her. "He says I'm bourgeois," Shauna told Todd.

"What's wrong with that?"

"I've got blood on my hands according to Danny."

To Todd her hands were small nude animals, defenceless and pink. Impulsively, he lifted one and kissed it. Shauna wanted to make Danny jealous, that was why she started sleeping with him.

Todd removes the cloth he's pressing hard against his forearm. The letters immediately write themselves in red—S-H-A-U—and dribble down the side of the basin. He feels woozy, but takes up the knife again, braces his arm on the sink, grateful he can do the *N* in three quick cuts and won't have to hack out another curve in his flesh.

Todd will heal, but he'll never wear short sleeves again.

The next day a police officer will come. Abby will call when she discovers that her bank account has been cleaned out and she can't get back to Saskatchewan.

"Let me get this straight. You wrote him cheques?" the officer will say.

"For the knives," Abby will confess. "And to cover the rent. He said he'd pay me back."

"And your arm, mate?" The officer points to Todd's bandaged forearm. "He have anything to do with that?"

"No," Shauna will cry, moved to love again by Todd's sacrifice. Todd and Shauna won't find out till the next day that they're penniless. "That was my fault. It's all my fault."

Todd will always consider himself blameless. He even volunteers to identify the villain once they've rounded him up.

But after every knife is drawn from the block and the blades and handles are dusted for fingerprints, the officer will turn to them and say, "Sorry, kids. These knives are clean."

# Mr. Justice

Unasleep and breathing hard, massive in my old twin bed, he hefts himself in the dark, onto his side, captive whale rolling in a tank. Pushes off the mattress, heaves legs over the side: a seated position achieved at last. He plants his feet but can't actually feel the carpet—he's numbed, numbed by diabetes. He gropes the headboard, preparing to stand. He must be filled with dread. Once up, he sways there listening then, hearing nothing, lurches cursing for the door.

There's a night light in the hall, the bathroom door ajar at the end. He hesitates before stepping out.

Nothing.

Emboldened, he takes a second cautious step, then a third, and like this he goes, one hand on the wall. If he proceeds slowly there is no sound except the hardwood responding to his weight, but his balance isn't great, especially in the dark. He stumbles.

*Click.*

Swings around, furious. No one! How many nights has this been going on? How many times tonight? I see it all as on a darkened stage, my father's progress to the toilet. The sound pursues him. *Click, click, click, click.* He locks the bathroom door, lifts the seat. I don't look. He's my father, but we're not close to say the least.

A dribble. A dribble for his aggravation.

When he opens the door my mother is standing there in her nightgown. "What the hell do you want?" he roars.

"What did you and Lachlan fight about?" She told me she thought that this was why he couldn't sleep, because I'd come over to the house and argued with him.

"None of your business."

"You've been up all night, Gerald."

"That's none of your business either."

Downstairs my brother Richie calls out, afraid. "Ma! Ma!"

"Now look what you've started," he tells her.

The click follows him back to my childhood room. My mother doesn't hear it. Or if she does, she doesn't say anything. He decides on the latter, that he isn't crazy, that we're trying to make him that way.

He still can't sleep. His throat is dry. There's a bad smell in the room. He feels feverish, tormented. Why a click? What is the significance of *click*? An impatient finger tapping the judicial bench? Has he made a wrong decision? Is this supposed to be his conscience?

The strange thing is he only hears it at night. In the morning it's his habit, a vestige from his ranching boyhood, to dress to the waist and go shirtless to the bathroom to shave and wash. I see him sitting on the edge of the bed in his underwear catching in his left hand a huge roll of midriff flesh to puncture with the needle. He pulls an ankle up onto the opposite knee and stuffs an argyle sock with his enormous bloated foot. He can hardly get the sock on. The shoe is just as bad and now, muttering over the slow passing of another hellish night, he limps to the door having failed yet again to notice what the problem actually is.

At seven-thirty he descends the stairs in his blue-black suit to find my mentally retarded brother holding his lips closed with his fingers. Richie is big, like Father, six foot two plus hair. He gives the impression that if he sat on his chair with his feet flat on the floor, his knees would lift the table. The rule at breakfast is Father has the first word. He maintains an imperious silence, his patriarchal right, even as my mother comes in with his plate of eggs, HP Sauce and the triangles of white toast in the rack the way he likes them, cold. "I hope you eventually got some sleep, Gerald," she tells him, flouting his decree. I imagine her adding with a long-suffering sniff, "We certainly didn't," and lifting the tea towel to her throbbing temple.

Richie releases his lips. "Can I tell him about Pontius Pilate now?"

"I know all about it," Father snaps.

Since Father has made an utterance, Richie is free to speak. He's memorized it word for word and likes to put on the different voices, a growl for Pontius Pilate, a falsetto for Jesus. "'Are you the King of the Jews?' 'That's what *you* say.' 'Your own people have brought you before me. What have you done?' 'My Kingdom is not of this world!'"

Father makes flatulent sounds with the HP bottle, pretending not to hear.

After breakfast, he puts on his overcoat and leaves with his briefcase in hand. He backs the Mercedes out of the garage and through the lane, still seething over Richie and the video my mother gave him. Probably he's likening himself to Christ, all the sacrifices he's made for his family, unappreciated, even mocked. The house next door was bought several years ago by an offshore family, Taiwanese I think, who live in it for two weeks of the year. A Shaughnessy mansion, it's their summer cottage and to give it that summery look they've painted the Tudor accents bright turquoise and mustard yellow. My father redoubles his curses at the sight of it.

The very next block gives him reason to rage. In Vancouver a demolition is always preceded by particular fencing around the trees, a two-by-four frame with orange plastic netting stapled to it. The bulldozer levels anything not surrounded by this eye-catching corral. The house in question, an old mansion similar to my parents', is being sacrificed to make room for a new mansion of potentially incongruous style and dubious taste. My father objects obstreperously to this trend. After 1997, when Hong Kong reverted to the Chinese, he hoped it would stop. The first deeds on Shaughnessy properties included a clause to prohibit resale to Orientals. He actually told me this.

He drives past the chestnuts on Connaught Drive shivering in their winter nakedness. When he reaches the corner, he hits the indicator. *Click, click, click, click.* On his right, Shaughnessy United Church. Surely it strikes him then that Pilate too was a judge.

He turns onto Thirty-third and, sweating profusely now, passes the stained glass nave. One shoe feels much tighter, as if his foot has grown inside it since he put it on. Light-headed, filled with that same nocturnal apprehension, he doesn't want to use the indicator again, but it's rush hour and the line of cars behind needs to know if he plans to turn or go straight. Someone honks. His hand lifts, seemingly in slow motion.

*Click,*

    *click,*

        *click.*


When I get home that afternoon Erica meets me at the door in her *We're Happy Because We Eat Lard* T-shirt and a pair of men's silk pyjama bottoms she got at Value Village. "Those might be my father's cast-off pyjamas," I tell her. Then, "Are you sick?" She should be at work.

Her apple cheeks corroborate her "No." There's the wineglass she's holding, too. "Lachlan. Your mother phoned." She practically sings it: "There's bad news!"

"It's not Richie, is it?" I know it's not. She wouldn't be acting like this.

She casts down guilty eyes. "I'll get dressed. We're supposed to meet them at the hospital."

"Hospital? When did she call?"

"This morning."

I go to the kitchen to retrieve my mother's message. The wine bottle is open on the counter. As well as the message Erica saved, there are six new ones, all from my mother. My father has had a car accident. He's had a stroke. He's had a stroke and a car accident. He needs to see me. I listen to each convoluting instalment staring out the window at the condominium across the alley entirely swathed in bright blue plastic. Three years ago our own building wore this same costume. Entire Vancouver neighbourhoods have. Ours is a city dreamed by Christo.

In the bedroom, Erica stands in her skin, uncommitted to the clothes lying on the bed. She looks at me. How to interpret her woozy expression? A mid-afternoon wine high or something more pleasantly animal? We haven't had sex in over a year. Long before that it ceased to be an expression of love or pleasure. It was work, complete with supervisors. I was half expecting to be unionized. If I want to communicate my affection now, I rub her feet. It makes her purr.

My father is lying in a hospital bed waiting for me. I wonder what he wants but Erica helps me out of my Canada Post issue and head-butts me onto the bed. My father can wait, I decide.

Afterward, we scramble to dress and run out to the car. As soon as we're on the road, Erica starts to cry. "I'm sorry," she says, going through all the pockets of her Gore-Tex for a tissue. "He's your father."

I have to tell her. I don't want her to find out when we get there. "He's all right. He's not going to die."

"She said he had a stroke," she argues. "She said he crashed the car."

"Into a hedge. Apparently he's fine."

"Oh." She leans back and closes her eyes. I don't know which she feels more acutely, disappointment or embarrassment.

"It's so tiring," she says a few blocks later.

"Really? I feel invigorated." Sex—it's as good as a long walk. I'd forgotten.

"Hating him. How do people live like this?"

When we are almost at the hospital, she asks me to stop somewhere so she can buy some licorice.

My mother and Richie are in the waiting room when we arrive. As soon as Richie sees Erica he runs to her bellowing sobs. My mother lights into me. "I've been calling all day!" I keep one jealous eye on Erica sunk in Richie's King Kong embrace. What is there to prevent him from one day crushing her with his wild love?

After a decade toiling at various arty things, Erica became a special needs teacher. She did her practicum in the day program Richie attends. Proudly he would show me his Pisa-like ceramic pencil holders, his wind chimes made of cutlery and driftwood. Erica, he explained, had assisted in their creation. Sometimes, to give my mother a break, I pick Richie up from the surreal playroom where he spends his days. I met his muse on one of these occasions and have been the third party in this triangle ever since.

It used to be a quadrilateral. Erica was living then with this guy, Peter Stone, unhappily it turned out, for Peter had become increasingly critical over the years. She told me this on a later occasion (I started picking Richie up regularly), the time she came with us to the high school where I take Richie to shoot baskets. She would only see me if Richie was there, because she was still with Peter. I resented Richie for this condition, as well as his taunting cumulus of brown curls. (Is there a more distancing wedge that can be driven between two brothers than one balding while the other prodigiously keeps his hair?) That was five years ago. Erica's layup: three balletic leaps, an arabesque, the ball soaring in an arc and missing.

Erica offers Richie the Twizzlers. "He's going to be all right."

"I like Nibs."

My mother hisses at me, "He might well lose his leg. He has gangrene."

I'm confused now.

"It wasn't a stroke. He blacked out."

Insulin shock.

"No," she tells me, because she probably thought the same thing. "Now they say he has an ulcerated foot. The bone's infected. He's been walking around for God knows how long with a *tack* stuck in his heel."

She looks so old without her makeup. I can't imagine her leaving the house without her face; probably the crisis washed it off. Her bob is grey, her complexion grey. Around her lined neck are her pearls. She's like an opened oyster, vulnerable, yet sympathy recoils from her. "Go and talk to him," she says.

"Where is he?"

"Second door on the right."

My father is going to live. Erica may have turned the ringer off, but I listened to all the hospital dispatches. That being the case, I could have *not* come. The last time I saw my father I vowed never to speak to him again.

"He did ask me to come, right?"

My mother glances at my knees. "It's winter, Lachlan. I wish you would wear long pants."

A private room, naturally. Beside the door, scrawled on a strip of cardboard and slid into a clear plastic track, is our name, the "Mr. Justice" dropped. I knock and, receiving no reply, nudge the door. The sight of him in a bed instead of behind a desk or at the head of the dinner table, in a straining hospital gown instead of suit-and-tied, is nothing short of shocking.

"Hey."

Slowly, he turns. He uses two handleless brushes on his hair. When I was a boy I used to sit on the edge of the tub and, in awe, watch him curry himself, both sides simultaneously. Now, sticky with Brylcreem, his hair stands on end, grey. Surgical tape spans the bridge of his nose, dotted in the centre an ignominious red. His dewlap sags.

"How are you feeling?"

He stares, the way he does when he considers a question too imbecilic to warrant a reply. To evade his terrible eye, I look around for a chair. It's right there. I sit and, still seeking refuge, scan the rest of the room. There's a window, the ledge bare. No one has sent flowers. Surely his cronies at the Court of Appeal could pitch in for a fruit basket. Yet I, his first-born son, have been equally remiss. My father is not a man who inspires the giving of gifts.

I try again at conversation. "What happened?"

He releases me to stare at the blank wall beyond the end of the bed. "Your mother told you all about it, I'm sure."

"She said something about a tack."

"She's trying to make me look like a fool."

"She's not. Didn't you feel it?"

"I *heard* it. I didn't know what the hell it was."

He works his mouth as though his tongue is restless. I wait for him to say something else. He doesn't. I wait for him to mention our argument a few days ago. To get it off his chest. He doesn't. I even wait for his usual barb, "How's Canada Post treating you?" The sounds of the hospital—cart rattlings, elevator pings—insinuate themselves. I hear his laboured respiration.

"Do you need anything?" I break down and ask.

"No."

"Mother and Richie are in the waiting room. Do you want me to tell them to come in?"

"Tell them to go home."

I'm so angry when I leave, I nearly punch the wall.

He never asked for me at all.

Four days later, my mother phones and asks us to come over. "You don't have to," I tell Erica, but uncomplaining, she accompanies me to Connaught Drive. She does it for Richie.

My mother is house-proud in the extreme. Not only does she not want anything dirtied or damaged, she wants the people who come into her home to match the decor. She doesn't approve of Erica's thrift-store style yet always has a ready compliment, thereby tainting everything she says with insincerity. Erica is from Saskatchewan. I think she reminds my mother that she hasn't always lived on Connaught Drive.

For our wedding four years ago Erica's mother sewed her a simple, pale blue dress. My mother took me aside after seeing it on a hanger. "No," she said.

"Her mother made it."

"It only goes to the knee."

"She doesn't want a long dress. That's not her."

"She doesn't shave, Lachlan." She gave me a cheque for three thousand dollars that she'd got my father to write. "You've got eighteen days." Already she'd declared that the wedding would be in a church, Holy Rosary Cathedral no less. Potluck? She'd shuddered. She invited two hundred people. We invited twenty.

At Value Village we picked out the most outrageous dress. It had dirigible sleeves and a yellow tag and as it happened to be a yellow day, we got forty percent off the thirty-five dollars. We had it dry cleaned and altered and no one guessed it had already been in the embrace of hundreds of well-wishing Greeks. Erica gleefully donated the balance of my father's money to various left-wing charities.

I worried about how Erica would get along with my mother after this, though I needn't have. My mother's devotion to Richie redeems her in Erica's eyes. Erica spends her working days in the company of the "mentally challenged." In her view her clients actually have more sense than the average person because they are trained to think through the consequences of their behaviour, to consider others as well as themselves, to be *moral*, while the rest of us, receiving no such instruction, act out of self-interest most of the time. She *expects* intelligent people to behave stupidly. It's not like her to hold a grudge either. She even invited her old boyfriend to the wedding, the same Peter Stone who used to ridicule her for taking the trouble to put toilet-paper tubes in the recycling and who once inflicted on her the indignity of gonorrhea.

When we arrive, Richie answers the door. He wants Erica to watch a video with him. "It's *The Greatest Story Ever Told!*"

"Is it? What's it about?"

"Jesus."

If Erica had made the movie this would be the story-line: a man and a woman go for a walk around the block pushing a baby carriage.

"Go watch your show, Richie," my mother tells him.

Erica says, "I don't mind."

"No. I want you to hear this too."

Erica and I wait in the living room while my mother prepares the drinks. Every few years she has the sofa and chairs reupholstered; she moves things around. I can never quite put my finger on what's different. Some of the furniture came with the house, the billiard table for example, which the house was built around. A portrait of my father looking severe and judgmental in his robes hangs above the fireplace. Down the hall, the video starts up midscore just as my mother carries in the tray.

"That's a pretty scarf." She hands Erica her soda water. "Please. A coaster. Pass her one, Lachlan." She leans back in the armchair that used to be another colour and, fingering her pearls, sighs. "The leg's coming off tomorrow."

"They warned you that would probably happen."

"There's a fifty percent chance he'll lose the other leg within five years. But that's not why I asked you to come."

"What's going on?"

"He's stepped down."

A cough explodes from Erica. "A coaster!" my mother practically shouts when Erica sets down her drink.

Bent forward hacking, Erica manages to shove the disc under the glass. "Sorry," she says, slapping her chest. "You said the leg was coming off, then that he—" She giggles. "—stepped down."

"From the bench," my mother says coldly.

"I understand. It just sounded funny."

"He's retiring." She turns to me, imploring. "What am I going to do?"

"He's sixty-eight. It's time."

"I can't have him home all day long, Lachlan! What do you think life around here is going to be like for us? He's not going to change."

He's not going to change. This is what we think. Neither can we conceive of our own lives being different. Everything we do has always been in relation to him.

Erica looks up and smiles at Richie filling the entire doorway. "What is it?" my mother snaps.

"My favourite part is coming up."

Erica makes her escape. As soon as she's out of the room, my mother leans forward in her chair. "What was it you spoke to your father about that night, Lachlan? You fought. Tell me what it was about."

The circumstances of my mother's life—looking after a son who, like in some Lewis Carroll nightmare, grows and grows while remaining perpetually six; serving (for that is what she does, thanklessly) my father, a difficult man to say the least—have forced her to seek refuge in faith. She's a daily communicant. Even if she were the kind of mother a grown son confides in, given the Church's stand, how could I tell her what had happened?

Before Erica and I got married we discussed having children. Erica wanted them, but wasn't in any hurry. "Let's just stop with the pill and see what happens."

What happened was she woke one night in agony. It was an ectopic pregnancy and Erica lost her tube on the left side. Then she got serious. She got us organized. Charts went up. First thing every morning she fellated the thermometer. She slowly drew apart a thumb and forefinger moistened with vaginal secretions, hoping for that wondrous string, clear and elastic, that signals ovulation. I had to stay in bed just in case. Lying there, I thought of my father's most scathing verdict: Richie and I were *useless*. For the first time in my life I felt essential.

Eight months later Erica underwent a procedure to flush her reproductive organs with dye. We saw for ourselves on the X-ray the clot of scars that blocked the remaining tube.

And so we went to see my father in his chambers downtown. At the Court Registry, I explained that I was the judge's son and shouldn't require an appointment. The clerk rang my father. "Your son. Yes. He says he's your son." She cupped a hand over the receiver. "What did you say your name was?"

Twenty minutes later a uniformed sheriff came to escort us up. He was armed.

My father takes great pride in the fact that he's "self-made." He might have stayed in Alberta; he was expected to take over the ranch. Instead he put himself through university by working in the oil patch during the summer. In the fifties, after graduating from law school, he married my mother and brought her to the coast where he'd joined a firm. My mother didn't want the nice new house in West Vancouver he offered to build her, but the one the realtor had shown them in Shaughnessy, subdivided during the war and allowed to fall to near ruin. There was a tree growing up through the foundation, bursting into leaf in the billiard room. While my mother pretends to be an English Lady, my father considers himself superior to his neighbours because hard work brought him to Connaught Drive, not privilege. He means his Caucasian neighbours. He feels superior to his Chinese neighbours for other reasons.

"I'm in court in an hour," he told us as we came in. "Couldn't you have come to see me at the house?"

"Not with Mother there." I took the chair on the other side of the massive desk. Erica stood with her back to us, pretending to examine the provincial crest.

I'd never asked him for money before. He'd paid for my under-graduate degree and would've paid for law school too, as well as helped me set up a practice. I'd known this my whole life, but had forfeited it. "We need a loan."

"What? Your good union wage isn't enough?"

"Ten thousand. Not all at once."

"What for?"

I told him about the ectopic pregnancy, our subsequent difficulties, the private clinic where we hoped to have the treatments. It had cost two hundred dollars just to attend an information session. We were still paying for the new vapour barrier in the condo. Erica has a student loan. He stared at his hands folded on the desk as he listened. I've never seen him in court but imagine that this is the pose he strikes on the bench.

His sole question: "What do you want children for?"

Erica held her tongue until the sheriff had escorted us back out. "That was the cruellest thing I have ever heard anyone say.

How could he say that to his own child? He wishes he'd never had you? It's bad enough how he treats you and Richie, but to say that to your face. Oh, my God!"

I wasn't offended. He'd said far worse. What struck me was the way he met my eye to ask me. I realized he hadn't actually looked at me in years. Or I hadn't looked at him.

"Do you ever imagine your funeral," Erica went on, crimson in my defence, "and wonder who'll come and what they'll say? When your father dies no one will even cry."

I thought of Erica's funeral, pews overflowing with the bobbing and drooling lives she's touched. I could afford to laugh. He'd written us a cheque.

My father's left leg is amputated just below the knee. Because of the danger of complications he's kept in the hospital until his transfer to the rehabilitation centre. When this happens, my mother presents me with a cellphone.

"It's to carry while you're at work. So I'll be able to get a hold of you."

"No," I tell her.

"Please. I'll only use it in case of emergency."

I don't believe she's capable of such restraint, but to her credit, my mother abides by the rules. She and Richie go to see my father every day. She waits until evening to call me at home and report his condition.

For years my route has been in Kerrisdale, the neighbourhood to the west of Shaughnessy, where I grew up. Like Shaughnessy, it's affluent. The streets are pretty and tree-lined, with many of the original stucco and shingle houses. This makes Kerrisdale an unusual neighbourhood in a city with a propensity for destroying and remaking itself. Because I grew up in an old house, and because I live now in Fairview Slopes where in the eighties virtually all of the original homes were demolished and replaced with leaky condos, I feel protective of the houses that remain. It's the houses I deliver the mail to, not the people, whom I hardly ever see. It's happening here too now. The dismay I feel climbing the steps to an Arts and Crafts bungalow, depositing *The New Yorker* and the *Architectural Digest* in the box, then turning and glimpsing from the corner of my eye an orange fence halfway down the block. Did I process a Change of Address? This was when I might have taken warning.

The cellphone rings and I answer to sobbing.

"He says he won't come home!"

It's my mother.

"Has he been discharged?"

"Ever! He says he's not coming back. He says he's going to move to Bowen. Go and talk to him. Please! I think he's lost his mind."

I stand on the sidewalk staring at a massive crater in the ground. A meteor might have crashed here, precisely in the centre of the lot. For the life of me I can't recall the vanished house.

I don't actually speak to my father when I go to see him in rehab that afternoon. He's not in his room. There's a plant on the sill (brought by my mother, no doubt) and his insulin kit on the bedside table. Pamphlets: *Choosing Your Prostheses*, *Wrapping Your Residual Limb*. A nurse stops in the doorway to tell me my father has just gone for physio. "Drop in," she says. "Cheer him on."

I find the room. My father, barely contained by the wheelchair, has his broad back to the open door. His hair is longer than I've ever seen it and, spared the sight of his meaty nape, I have to look twice to recognize him. The physio, a middle-aged, pear-shaped woman in a track suit, asks questions off a clipboard. "How's the pain today, Gerry?"

*Gerry?*

I freeze in the doorway. My father the judge, *Gerry*? I can't make out his reply. I doubt he condescends to offer one. He must be staring at her, the way he stares at store clerks who have the temerity to ask, "How are you today?" The way he stares at us. The oblivious physio tosses the clipboard on the desk behind her and, smiling witlessly, holds out her arms for her comeuppance. My father fumbles for the crutches that are leaning against the wall. When he has succeeded in hoisting himself out of the chair, he pauses to rest. My sense of foreboding mounts. As soon as he gets within a crutch's length of her, he's going to let her know just who isn't Gerry. I don't think I can bear to watch.

"Wonderful, Gerry. That's just great."

My father takes a step.

"Beautiful!"

With his every lurch forward, the physio takes a step back. Nothing else happens. I'm confused for the moment it takes me to recognize what is actually going on. Erica too is in a helping profession. She treats my brother Richie, who was once partially in her care, with this same seemingly selfless loving-kindness. "Gerry" responds as Richie does with Erica, eager to please, to reciprocate, crutching toward the open-armed physio. He's wearing a navy pullover and, now that the wheelchair no longer blocks my view, I see the incongruity of pale blue cotton hospital pants. On the right side, his thick black-socked ankle rides in the huge boat of his slipper. I'm completely unprepared for the empty space between the hem of the left pant leg and the floor, the nothingness. I stare as though at the desecrated statue of a deposed tyrant, as though I am seeing *through* some part of him. I can hardly believe that some piece of my monumental father is missing.

Later that night, before I've thought of an excuse to give my mother for bolting from the rehab centre, she calls with more news. She's received a letter.

"From Father?" I ask.

"From his lawyer."

"He has a *lawyer*?"

My father's petition for divorce sends my Catholic mother to her bed for a week. I'm delegated to pick up Richie from his program. "Where's Ma?" he asks, every day suspicious.

"She's not feeling well. Let's go shoot some baskets."

"Bye Richie!" one of the workers calls. The Human Parrot does her thing. "Bye Richie Bye Richie Bye Richie Bye Richie Bye Richie Bye Richie!" She suffers from some avian syndrome: small head, tiny close-set eyes, beak. As we leave, she stomps around the door, wingless.

Richie shuffles to the car dragging his Canucks lunch kit. "Where's Ma?"

I have to move the passenger seat back before he gets in, way back, and even then push his head against his chest so he doesn't brain himself on the door frame. "She's at home. She's not feeling well."

We drive over to Point Grey High where a group of kids is already on the asphalt. Their bagging jeans nearly drop every time they take a shot. This does not look very cool to me. Richie carries the basketball against his stomach. Without him, I probably wouldn't venture over to a potential youth gang and suggest we share the court, but my brother has an effect on people. He parts a crowd, like Jesus. The kids decide right away to abort their game and walk off with their backpacks and Big Gulps, holding up their pants.

I do the legwork, dribbling, feinting. Richie stands on one spot and waits for me to pass him the ball. No matter where he stands, he scores. In this small regard, he's a savant. He's NBA material. But this week he's feeling too insecure to enjoy himself. "I want to go home," he announces before I've even worked up a sweat.

Erica takes the evening shift during the crisis. My mother's collapse seems to lift her from her own depression—or maybe it just takes her mind off things. Every night she goes over to keep Richie company, but when I offer to keep her company keeping him company, she declines. She takes a tray in to my mother. She asks how my mother is feeling. Apparently it's been years since anyone asked my mother this because she's confiding in Erica now and may not with me around.

When I take the ferry over to see my father, he's been living on Bowen Island for a month. We have a cabin there, but haven't used it as a family for years. In adolescence Richie developed a fear of water. He flaps his hands and rocks and moans, so can't be taken on the ferry without unsettling the other passengers. Since then, my father has taken the short trip alone two or three times a year.

Both my mother and Erica asked me to go. It's a warm June morning, so I stay on deck with the car and from halfway across Howe Sound can see the long bank of Point Grey and the silhouetted towers of the university. The island seems a stone's throw away, humpbacked and green. I haven't spoken to my father since that afternoon in the hospital last winter. A few days before that, I'd gone to see him at the house. This was when we had our fight.

I found him in his study off the billiard room on the main floor where he hides from Richie and my mother. At first he wouldn't answer my knock. "What do you want?" he finally barked. Seeing it was me, he looked surprised, then, rightly, suspicious. "Oh. You must need money."

I laughed.

"I don't recall you've paid me back for the last loan."

Did he even remember what it was for? Two years had gone by. "We've saved about half of it," I told him, "but now our plans have changed." He returned to his reading. I pressed on. "We're not asking you for more money. We're asking the bank. But if you would co-sign the loan and give us an extension on paying you back."

"What's wrong with you? You're an adult. You're supposed to make your own way in the world, not keep coming to your father for an allowance. You made a decision against my better judgment not to pursue any kind of career. Now you come crawling to me for these handouts. No one gave me a handout, let me tell you." He said all this without lifting his eyes from the page he was reading.

"Erica's forty."

"What has that got to do with anything?"

I didn't expect him to understand. "We'd like to adopt."

Now he reared up. "Are you mad? You want to take on someone else's crack-addled bastard?"

"I'm sure Erica would, but unfortunately it would take too long."

"I see those people every day. I put them in jail."

"We'd like to pursue an international adoption. There are fees."

"International," he said.

"China."

I thought he was going to say, "Connaught Drive, the new Chinatown," or bring up the Shaughnessy leases. Instead he leaned back in the chair and looked at me—*again*! "What do you want children for?" This time, he was not being rhetorical.

The fact is I don't want children. I hated being a child and having to look out for and cede to my brother at the same time I was expected to achieve for both of us. It would give me no pleasure to put someone else through that. I'm afraid a child of mine would turn out like Richie. Afraid of the kind of father I might be. I'm afraid *of* children. On my route I pass a playground and I can't help overhearing how inordinately concerned the underaged are with justice. *No fair! My turn! Liar!* I don't think I could live with a Utopian underfoot all day long.

"It would make Erica happy," I told my father.

"Divorce her."

"What?"

"Divorce her. You have grounds."

During the fertility treatments, I had to give Erica her injections. Her scrunched-up face and little yelp nearly demolished me each morning. Everything scientifically monitored, timed to the hour, I sat at her side in the clinic, holding her hand, hating the doctor with his face between her stirrupped legs for knowing deeper parts of her than I did.

A nurse led me off to a room not much bigger than a closet. Recliner chair, TV, selection of T. & A. on a side table. She opened the door of the cabinet the TV sat on and showed me how the VCR operated. "Here are the videos if you need them."

I scanned the labels. "Do you have *The Greatest Story Ever Told?*"

My mother tells me that the thing she finds most exhausting about caring for Richie is keeping him from touching himself. When we were children, she was fiercely vigilant on this account. I glanced at the magazines, but was uninspired. Where to look? If I closed my eyes, I pictured my mother wagging a finger at me. Down the hall, they were extracting Erica's carefully cultivated eggs for me to fertilize. Along with the pain of the injections, she'd had to endure daily ultrasounds and blood tests, headaches, fatigue, bloating, my mother mentioning three times at Sunday dinner, "Erica, I do believe you're putting on weight." All that was required of me was to produce a tablespoon of jism.

I tried a video but couldn't figure out the story.

In the end I settled on Erica, as I would the whole next year we were celibate. Before I met her, I used to read the personal ads to learn what other men actually thought of themselves. I am *WM, 5' 10", bald, lacks self-worth, ambition*. I might have ended up like my brother, on Connaught Drive forever, except that Erica married me.

My epitaph: *Here lies a man who masturbated to the thought of his own wife.*

And my father advised me to divorce her.

Exactly what we yelled at each other I don't recall. My mother met me at the door and tried to stop me from leaving. "I didn't even know you were here. What is going on?"

Normally, I'm not so foolish as to get into an argument with a judge.

The ferry bumps into the Snug Cove dock. It's been more than twenty years, yet as I drive off I see that, though the village has been tarted up for tourists, the old library is still there and even the Bow-Mart coffee bar where Richie and I, spooning sundaes, used to jostle each other on the stools. Surprising that I know the way, turning onto Bowen Bay Road as though I've actually driven here before. These hills and curves I've travelled only in a back seat, growing queasier and queasier until, reaching the cabin, I threw up in the driveway.

I leave the car in the public parking area and walk up the road dense on both sides with ferns. Looking up at the trees invites vertigo. The cabin is exactly as I remember it, but for the thicker thatch of moss and the paint peeling like arbutus bark. I climb the three wooden steps up to the porch.

I never came back because I didn't want to spend a weekend alone with my father. He's expecting me now. I called ahead. When I see him through the screen coming to answer my knock, I realize that what I feel is dread. I'm both afraid of him and afraid of seeing him lamed, though the latter makes no sense considering all the times I've cut him down in my mind. Though limping, he moves at a fair pace with his cane. When he pushes open the screen and stands aside to let me in, I see that he's given up for good his biweekly visits to the barber. He's lost weight, too, thirty pounds at least, not counting what the leg weighed.

"You look great," I say, not daring to look down.

Astonishing, the thing he does. He lifts the left leg to show me—khaki pant leg, brown sock, leather loafer. It looks real, except when he strikes it with the cane I hear a plasticky thump. The astonishing thing is he grins.

Inside, I'm subsumed with nostalgia. The mildewy smell of the cabin, the yellow and brown plaid sofa, coffee table piled with old fishing magazines, though the fish are gone now. The orange net curtain on the window, driftwood and shells crowding the ledge. It's clean. He must have hired someone. I wonder about the cooking because, as far as I know, my father has never cooked a meal in his life. Glancing through the pass-through window to the kitchen, I see, along with all the old appliances, a microwave and some very shiny pots in the draining rack beside the sink.

"Drink?"

I nod and he canes his way to the sideboard still jammed with board games for us to play on rainy days, though Richie mostly threw the cards around. "You're managing?"

He smiles again, slyly. "I am."

I'm confused by these smiles. He seems almost gleeful, and all at once I understand: he's trying to prove a point. He wants to show that he can tackle these domestic chores, and on one leg, simply to nullify the claims my aggrieved mother has made. These smiles are about the divorce.

He hands me the whiskey. "What ferry are you taking back?"

"The 3:05, I think."

"The 2:05 will be less crowded."

"That doesn't give me much time."

"Time for what?"

"I'd like to look around. It's been a while."

"What does your mother want?"

"To know how you're doing."

He makes a familiar sound through his nose, an exhalation of contempt. "Come out on the deck."

The sliding door is open. He goes ahead, startling a hummingbird off the hourglass feeder that hangs from the tree beside the deck. A flare, metallic green, an angry squeak—the bird buzzes off. It's so much brighter than inside the cabin I have to shade my eyes. Side by side, leaning on the deck railings, we look out over the bay dotted with coloured buoys. Pasley, Gabriola, Vancouver—the islands recede in lighter shades of grey.

"I'm going to build a new cabin," he announces.

"Where?"

"Here. I'm going to tear this one down."

I feel an actual pang.

"You can tell your mother that. Go down and look at what they built on the old Pederson place. Go on. I can't negotiate the beach yet."

The stairs from the deck are half rotted. In the grassy fringe around the bay the rowboats and kayaks lie with their keels to the sky. I step over the driftwood logs that have washed in during the winter and scrunch along the sand. Though I don't remember where the Pederson place was, I see a new cabin, all blond wood and glass, a modern take on the traditional longhouse.

The tide is out. For a while I nose around on the beach and search the crevasses between the rocks, clogged purple with starfish orgies. I find flat stones to skip. These were Richie's and my childhood occupations. We also liked to bury each other.

"You'd better hurry if you're going to catch the 2:05!" my father calls.

When I'm back on the deck stamping the sand off my shoes, he asks me, "What do you think?"

"We had fun here."

"Of the Pederson place."

There's a fifty percent chance he'll be legless in five years. There's also a fifty percent chance he'll be dead. These are the statistics my mother has relayed to me.

"Impressive," I say.

Before my father hurries me out, I use the bathroom. I want to take one last look in the bedrooms too, but both doors are closed. I would even drive around the island, then catch the 3:05 as planned, if I could be sure that Erica had a good day.

I depend on antidepressants, currently Paxil. My mother has that other drug, religion. But Erica insists she'll work through her feelings in her own good time. For now she's angry and bitter and disappointed. She thinks my father refused to help us with the adoption out of spite. Principle, I told her, not spite. He's a judge. In law, spite—indeed all the things we feel now—is irrelevant. My father has no feelings. Certainly he's never concerned himself with how his family feels, nor demonstrated any more emotion for Richie and me than he would for two tablespoons of jism.

The picture above the toilet is missing; the nail hole and the darker rectangle of yellow betray the absence. I don't remember what was there. A photograph? I wash and dry my hands then open the medicine cabinet. This is when I realize how wrong we are, that he has, in fact, remade himself precisely because of something that he feels. Calamine lotion, Dettol, Band-Aids are the things I expect and indeed hope to see, but the balms of my childhood summers have been cleared out and replaced by mouthwash, deodorant, a profusion of prescription bottles, lancets, needles. When I close the cabinet, the mirror confronts me. Deep parenthetical lines cut my face, the scars of a perpetual frown.

My father is happy. This is why he smiles.

"Well?" Erica asks when I get in. Freshly showered, she passes me in the hall, a solemn Bedouin. In the bedroom she gets into bed, removes the towel and begins combing out her wet hair.

When I tell her what I've concluded, she hurls the comb. It smarts against my shoulder. "Ow."

"He's happy? That's just swell. But what about his shattered family? What about our *unhappiness*? I can't believe you didn't tell him off. Why don't you stand up to him? I can't stand how passive you are! You're hopeless! The lot of you!"

She thinks I'm passive? Well, *that* hurts. All my life I've struggled. It took no small effort to fail at every goal he set for me. It was a test of wills. I won.

Just look at me.

At dinner on Connaught Drive that night I ask Richie if he remembers going to Bowen Island. He interrupts the painstaking sawing of his meat to look up.

"Don't remind him," my mother says.

We are arranged as usual along the twelve feet of waxed mahogany, Erica and I on one side, Richie and my mother on the other, my father's place at the head, in the only chair with arms, the throne, empty. What is my father doing now, I wonder. Microwaving his dinner and eating it out of the plastic tray?

My mother asks, "Did you talk to your father, Lachlan? Did you talk to him about it?"

"About what?"

"You *know* what." She points her chin at my brother counting to ten over and over in his head as he chews. (I know because I once asked what he thought about while he ate that made him look so stern.) We are forbidden to utter the D-word in his presence.

"No," I tell her.

Erica sits with her elbows on the table, pressing her temples. "Isn't that the whole reason you went over?"

Sarcasm again? I don't think I like this new mother-and-daughter-in-law alliance.

"I don't want him back," my mother says. "Did you tell him that?"

Richie remembers. "I'm scared on the ferry!"

"As far as I'm concerned it's good riddance. He can go to the Canary Islands for all I care."

"Are we going on the ferry?"

Erica tells him, "No."

"But why D-I-V-O-R-C-E?"

"Erica?" says Richie. "Do you want to watch a video after dinner?"

"I do, Richie. I'd love that."

"It's *The Greatest Story Ever Told*."

"Why not a legal separation? Why isn't that good enough? Does he hate us so much?"

The cutlery makes pained sounds against the Royal Doulton.

"How can you live with someone for forty years then walk out without an explanation?" my mother says a minute later.

An animal caught in a trap will chew its leg off: this comes to me in a flash.

"It's unconscionable," Erica agrees.

"*Over* forty years."

"But the thing is, he's not here anymore." Erica points to his chair. "Look. He's gone. He's rid of us, but we're not rid of him."

"When is Daddy coming back?" Richie asks.

Erica gets up and comes around the table. With Richie looking on in alarm, she takes his plate, his spoon and knife and glass of milk and carries it all to the head of the table, where she lays it out. "Sit here, Richie."

Fork clutched in fist, he shrinks right down to the size of a normal man. We stare at him, hopeful he will save us. Richie begins to rock. The hand not holding the fork rises and flaps beside his stricken face.

"Oh, never mind." Erica turns and stalks out of the room.

My mother looks at me, startled by this flagrant breach of etiquette.

"She's depressed," I explain.

"Erica told me what you and your father fought about that night, Lachlan. Why didn't you come to me?"

"For money?"

"Yes. I'll give it to you. When it happens—" She draws the *D* in the air. "We'll have to sell the house. I'll get half."

Tonight Erica sleeps soundly for the first time in months while I lie awake. I'm thinking about my father and how, when he first developed diabetes, the medical paraphernalia fascinated me. In my mid-twenties at the time, I was still living on Connaught Drive, unable to find a job that required the skills of an Honours English grad. I would sneak into my parents' room (either they still shared a bed or my father believed I had proprietary rights to my old room) and open the drawer of the bedside table where he kept his lancets and needles. He wouldn't speak to me because I'd flunked the LSAT. In some way I felt avenged by the sight of these small implements that gave him pain.

I wonder what he feels now.

Out on Bowen Island, he sinks down on the edge of the bed. The old mattress buckles as though he's getting into a rowboat. He pitches and laughs. Using the prosthetic foot as a lever, he slips the loafer off his real foot, rucks up the left pant leg far enough to get at the straps. The unfastened prosthesis falls onto its side on the braided rug. A dull thump.

Does he miss us? Is he nostalgic for us, for his former life, his past? Will he ever feel a pang, an ache, a throb, for what he's cut himself off from? And we, will we continue to feel the pain of a phantom father now that he's really gone?

It's night, the room dark. I can't see what isn't there, the missing leg, not even the stump. I can't visualize the stump sock tossed on the floor, or the man, Mr. Justice, my father the judge, Gerald, massaging the knob of flesh under the knee joint.

Gerry.

Who?

I don't know any such person.

# Shhh:
# 3 Stories About Silence

1

There was this man who worked for something like thirty years at the BBC. In the production side of things. Editing, cataloguing, filing. These were the days before computers and DAT, obviously. Everything was tape and spools. It was his job to edit out the ahs and ums, the fucks and Freudian slips, all that. Also the silences. When the pauses got too long—chop chop. In those thirty years he took the silences out of some mighty mouths. Khrushchev and Kennedy. Reagan and Gorbachev. The Beatles, Beckett, Nureyev. But he never met or interviewed these people himself. He was a stutterer.

So thirty years go by and the guy's old and he retires. They throw a party for him in the BBC canteen or somewhere. They ask him how it feels to have polished the voice of history. G-g-g-g-g-g, he says. Something like that.

All those years he'd kept the stuff he cut out. He had it all filed away and when he left, he took the files. He went to live in the country where it was quiet so he could work undisturbed. He had a project he'd been thinking about for years. Maybe in the beginning he planned to use the ums and fucks, but later he tossed them. It was the silence he was interested in. What Reagan didn't say. What Kissinger sounded like when he finally shut the fuck up. He spliced these together, but not just in any old order. He was working with different qualities and textures in the silence. He was a composer, right?

Now and then he played the tapes for people. They found them profoundly moving. Some were reduced to, you know. Tears.


2


And?

He died a few years later.

What happened to the tapes?

Eric turns on the ignition long enough for the back windows to purr and descend. I don't know.

Where did you hear about him?

On the radio.

Nat starts to laugh. Eric of all people tells this story with reverence? He hasn't shut up since they got in the car, not for the forty-minute drive to the terminal, not for the twenty minutes they've been cooking in the ferry lineup. Opinions he's got, and anecdotes, but mostly facts, facts, facts, like he's shaking his teeming brain out in her lap.

He leans back. Sticks his hand up through the open sunroof into the blue of Horseshoe Bay. Sunlight sheers off his Medic Alert bracelet. Lifestyles's not so bad, he says. I could get used to this. I could get used to fee-jords.

Fjords, says Nat.

I know. But I didn't always. I mean, *f* and *j*. *F* and *j* together?

There's only one other word in the English language that starts with *f* and *j*.

Nat says nothing.

Aren't you curious?

She sighs.

Fjeld. A high, rocky plateau, especially in Scandinavia. There she is.

The ferry emerges from behind a green meringue, plowing the blue, a toy still, but growing larger. We'd better get on, says Nat, desperate now, but this is not entirely certain. Cars, minivans, motorcycles, SUVs, recreation vehicles—they all infarct the lanes. She's beginning to think along the lines of unlikely and two more talkie hours with the encyclopedic Eric. She hardly knows him. Like her, he's not on his usual beat, accidents and crime scenes. Nat returned six months early from mat leave and couldn't get City Hall back. It's Lifestyles all summer for Nat.

Eric says, Boats are feminine in English but masculine in French.

Yeah? I'm going to *la toilette*.

You'd better hurry.

Outside the car she pauses to adjust her skirt, which has been taking its own ride. She slings her purse strap over her shoulder and walks off into the hot metal maze of cars. When she glances back, she happens to catch Eric in a frank act of appreciation. It's her he's appreciating. He looks away and so does Nat, who can't remember the last time lust factored into her life. So thrown off balance, she has to put a hand on the hood of a truck to steady herself. It feels like a stove element.

In the grim portable that is the bathroom she takes a good look at herself, pleasant enough when she smiles, but she can't have been doing that. She splashes her face, dries it with paper towels, puts on lipstick. Then the voice of doom announces that the ferry has docked. Straightening, she sees them in the mirror, her obvious selling point—the twin trophies of a nursing mother.

When she gets back to the car Eric asks, How's Don? as though this will retract the appraising look. It doesn't. It has fully penetrated and is marauding around inside her.

Better.

What was the matter exactly?

Panic attacks.

When's he coming back?

She keeps her gaze forward, pretending to watch the chain reaction of brake lights in all the lanes as the engines start up. It's not enough to be able to leave the house, she says. He's a cartoonist. He has to get his sense of humour back.

I love his stuff, Eric says. But can you explain the hedgehog?

The what?

The hedgehog. What's the significance?

Eric is actually attractive in a dissolute way, she realizes now. He has tons of silver-threaded hair, which he wears long with his tan and his crumpled paper bag of a linen shirt. Hiding behind his Euro sunglasses, morning-after eyes. What are you talking about? she asks.

There's that nasty hedgehog in all his cartoons.

Oh. That's not a hedgehog. That's his Self-loathing.

Their lane begins to move. Neither of them speaks, though this can hardly be called silence. A man in an orange vest stops the fourth car ahead of Eric's.

Oh well, says Nat. She smiles. Now what are we going to do with ourselves?

The man confers briefly with the radio clipped to his vest, then begins paddling the air toward himself. The line advances.

Eric's is the last car on.

Ronald Reagan received a life-sized topiary elephant for his eighty-second birthday.

Really? She notices herself in his sunglasses, wearing her sunglasses, head cocked, feigning interest.

It weighed as much as an actual elephant and took eight years to grow.

They are sitting out on deck watching the fjords recede, the wind an unrelentingly fond uncle tousling their hair. It inflates the baggy clothes of a nearby group of teens. They look blown-up, like they could float away. Nat left her jacket in the car and she shivers in her sleevelessness.

There's a topiary zoo in Portsmouth, Rhode Island.

Do birds kiss? Nat asks.

What?

She points to the ferry's bronze bell where two crows perch, apparently swapping spit. Her phone rings in her purse. When she sees it's Don, she tells Eric, I'm going to get some batteries from the gift shop. She walks away, out of earshot, wondering about panty lines.

Don asks, How are things?

I'm on the ferry. Is everything all right?

Yeah.

Did you talk to him?

Not yet.

There is a pause. (This, Nat thinks, should be edited out.)

I will when Gemma goes down, Don says.

Nat says, I'll call you when we're heading back.

He hesitates.

(This too.)

Bye.

Bye.

She finds Eric in line at the cafeteria, marvels to see his lips are moving. He brightens at her approach, takes off his sunglasses

*141*

and hooks them over his chest hair. She chooses V8 and a salmon sandwich.

A sockeye can jump thirty-two feet, Eric tells her. He orders a B.C. burger.

How high can a cow jump? Nat asks.

While they're eating, he tells her about the garden in Columbus, Ohio.

Stop, she begs. You've been doing research. You're making me look bad.

In Columbus, Ohio, they've recreated Seurat's *Un dimanche après-midi à l'île de la Grande Jatte*. In topiary. I saw the pictures. It's amazing.

A piece of his spittle flies across the table and lands on her. It's warm, but it cools immediately. How long till she can wipe it off without his noticing? It sits there, a tiny weight on her cheek, the spit of the former most annoying man in the world.

*The Beachcombers* lasted nineteen seasons. Three hundred and some episodes.

They're driving through Gibsons Landing. Eric points out Molly's Reach, the pub featured in the beloved TV series. Just think. People in Costa Rica and Slovenia, all over the world where *The Beachcombers* is still in reruns, they know this pub.

I wonder if we'll see a Bruno Gerussi topiary, says Nat, and Eric laughs. Since they've gotten back in the car, the flirting has intensified, or so it seems to Nat. When he shifts gears, he grazes the side of her bare leg. Sorry, he said the first time.

Once they're clear of Gibsons, the drive is prettier. On Eric's side the ocean sometimes insinuates itself into the view between the rocks and trees. That's *Arbutus menziesii*, he says, pointing out a tree on a rocky ledge above them.

Bark hangs off its trunk in long cinnamon strips, like a skin disease. Nat asks, What's the matter with it?

They're in moult.

They pass a golf course, a nursery, numerous hand-painted signs that point up narrow gravel roads, like the one they're looking for. *Herbs. Eggs. Massage Therapy.* At every bus stop some civic-minded resident has left a chair—a vinyl kitchen chair, a folding lawn chair, a resin patio chair, even two.

Nat opens the glove compartment, sees a box of condoms. The sandwich inside her leaps. She makes a show of looking. Map?

In the door, he says.

Ah. She slams the compartment. Just then they pass an inn. Oh God, she thinks. Condoms. An inn. On the way back, the interview will be shorthanded into her notebook, the topiaries locked in the chip in Eric's camera. They'll stop at the inn for a drink. They'll deserve it. Eric must be a vocal lover. She imagines him telling her how many sperm swim in a teaspoon of cum, how many orgasms a woman is capable of achieving compared to a man, while these things are happening.

Are you religious?

Nat starts at the question, not just because it annihilates her fantasy.

Sorry, says Eric. Maybe that's too personal a thing to ask.

No. She tugs her skirt down over her knees. I'm not.

For several minutes they drive without speaking. This is less of a relief than she would have thought back in the ferry lineup. She feels awkward, embarrassed even. Speaking of religion, she finally says. We're out in Surrey now. We bought an old farmhouse last year. There's a field out back where there used to be a barn. Someone approached Don and asked to put a trailer out there. Rent the field, he meant. Don knew the guy in high school so he said yes. Turns out he's part of this cult. There are people coming and going all the time.

How do you know it's a cult?

They do their thing out in the field. They walk around in a circle. Rain or shine they're out there walking. They owe us five months' rent.

The sign on the highway: *Topiaries*. They come to a second sign at the foot of a long driveway and turn there, raising dust. Nat rings at the house while Eric unloads his equipment from the trunk. It's an ordinary house, a seventies split-level painted green with a textured panel of amber glass beside the door. The garden in front is carnival coloured.

This is annoying, she tells Eric, who is waiting by the car now with his camera cases and tripod. I talked to her yesterday.

Maybe she's in the back.

She follows Eric around the side of the house through a trellis tunnel. The backyard opens into a large rectangular clearing cut out of the forest. Unlike the front, it's monochrome, carpeted with lawn. The topiaries, a dozen or more, stand on their own, connected by a bark mulch path.

Wow, says Eric, setting his equipment on the patio. He strikes off toward the closest figure while Nat calls out, Hello! Hello! She drops her purse on the patio table, takes out her notebook and phone, looks up the contact name and number, dials. A phone starts ringing inside the house.

She crosses the grass to where Eric is circling the Buddha. I can't believe this.

They haven't put up any signs, says Eric. Who's that over there? Jesus? Signs would help.

She catches sight of someone at the far side of the clearing emerging from the trees. Oh, thank God. She heads for him, waving. Hello! It's Natalie Koerner! From the *Sun*!

He disappears behind one of the figures. As she's cutting across the grass toward him, he dodges back into the trees. Hey! Nat yells. I saw you!

Gandhi, it looks like, when she reaches the topiary. A rake leans against his dhoti, clippings scattered at his feet. The man comes out of the trees again and pretends to be surprised to see her.

Very funny, she says.

He's young, not even twenty, wearing a baseball cap with an acronym, the same baggy clothes as the kids on the ferry, Nikes. Also work gloves, which bring the size of his hands into proportion with the size of his feet. His face is angular, gaze skitting. She gets the feeling he's listening hard, but not to her. Without even seeing the wires that connect him to it, she figures it out. A Discman.

I'm Natalie Koerner, she says, louder now, to compete with Eminem. From the *Sun*. I'm here to do an interview. An interview!

His face comes alive in a frown.

I set this all up yesterday with a woman named Joyce Pollard. Is she around?

He heaves a clownish shrug.

Are you the gardener? Or possibly the mime?

He emits a startling sound, like a seal's truncated bark, and signs beside his ear.

Fuck, says Nat, swinging round. Heedless of the path again she marches back to Eric.

The surrounding trees smell sugary in the heat. It's so quiet Nat can hear their cones snap open and the dry rain of seeds they release. The topiaries hold their stations, perfectly still, like green snow people. She's never seen anything so kitschy.

She's not here and that guy's deaf, she tells Eric.

He's standing before a green Mother, or some other, Theresa, sunglasses pushed to the top of his head. Eric usually takes pictures of dragged lakes, bland suburban houses encircled in yellow tape, the sculptural obscenities of highway smash-ups. She thinks he's figuring out his shot.

Across the garden the deaf boy's rake scratches the earth.

I don't have a story if I don't have an interview.
Eric tells her, Shhh.


## 3


PANEL: WOMAN IN A WHEELCHAIR, HEAD BANGING AGAINST HEADREST,
MOUTH STRETCHED TO THE SIDE. TERROR? MAN PUSHING, RED-FACED,
BIBBED WITH PERSPIRATION, OBVIOUSLY STRAINING TO KEEP THE CHAIR
ON THE PATH. DON AND GEMMA THE TALKING BABY WATCH FROM THE FENCE.
DON'S BALLOON: ROUGH RIDE!

Don hasn't actually set foot on the path himself, but he can see
that after a wet spring and an abnormally hot dry summer, it's a
lumpy circuit of hardened mud.

PANEL: GEMMA THE TALKING BABY STANDING ON THE FENCE, POINTING AT
THE WHEELCHAIR. PLENTY O' DROOL. GEM'S BALLOON: HEY! DIDN'T MA SAY
SOMETHING ABOUT LEGAL LIABILITY?

PANEL: BLAKE ALDERSON, SLEEVES ROLLED, BRINGING UP THE REAR. HIS TAT-
TOOS LOOK LIKE BURNS. GEM'S BALLOON: HERE HE COMES, POPS! SAY SOME-
THING! SAY SOMETHING!

PANEL: GEMMA BOUNCING ON THE FENCE, POINTING FRANTICALLY. DROOL
SPLASHING EVERYWHERE. DON'S SELF-LOATHING RUBS ITS SPINES AGAINST
THE FENCE.

This late in the day it's just the three of them, though sometimes as many as five are on the path at a time, evenly spaced,
presumably so they don't step on each other's heels and break
stride. On weekends extras sit cross-legged in the grass or on
their knees, praying while they wait to rotate in. Gemma prefers

them to *Teletubbies* so Don brings her down every day after her afternoon nap and stands her on the fence. She applauds and points and chortles in a knowing way, but not once has any of them smiled back or waved or so much as looked at her. This is how Don knows their God is not his.

PANEL: BLAKE ALDERSON GETTING CLOSER. DON LOOKS OVER HIS SHOULDER. DON'S BALLOON: HEY! IS THAT MA'S CAR? GEMMA THE TALKING BABY TEARS AT HIS HAIR. HER BALLOON: TALK TO HIM! DROOL RAINS DOWN AND DRENCHES THEM ALL. DON'S SELF-LOATHING PUTS UP A MINIATURE UMBRELLA.

Gemma protests being taken away by ripping the sun hat off her head. Mommy's home, Don tells her. He swings her onto his shoulders. Fat thighs squeeze his neck, the softest vise. She takes the reins.

Not so tight. Daddy doesn't have hair to spare.

PANEL: INSIDE, STRIPS OF WALLPAPER HANG OFF THE WALLS. A RAT CHASES DON'S SELF-LOATHING. GEMMA THE TALKING BABY RIDES IN ON DON'S SHOULDERS. MA GLARES OUT THE BEDROOM DOOR AT DON. DON'S THOUGHT BALLOON: SHE SEEMS EVEN MORE PISSED OFF THAN USUAL!

They find Nat changing out of her work clothes in the bedroom. Did you talk to him? she asks.

He lies so easily he surprises himself. Yes.

And?

He said they'd pay.

When?

Soon.

Not good enough. What were his exact words?

Don, stained with embarrassment, recites the platitude. The Lord will provide.

Ha! Nat snorts. Don't we get *any* credit?

Don takes Gemma to the kitchen for a drink.

PANEL: DON AND GEMMA THE TALKING BABY IN THE KITCHEN, THE SUN SHIN-
ING THROUGH A HOLE IN THE CEILING. A FILE OF CARPENTER ANTS MARCHES
DOWN A CUPBOARD DOOR IN TINY HARD HATS, SAWS OVER THEIR SHOUL-
DERS. ANTS' BALLOON: HEY, HO! HEY, HO! GEM'S BALLOON: WHAT'S EATING
MA? DON'S BALLOON: NOT YOU. SO IT'S GOT TO BE . . .

After an extensive search, the sippy cup is located under all the
dishes in the sink, filled with water and handed up. Gemma brings
it down on Don's head, hard—ow! Then Nat comes in, T-shirt
straining, and levels a displeased eye on the mess. What have you
been doing all day?

Looking after Gemma.

The anger slides right off her face when he says this. It's as
though she's just remembered she has a baby. She pulls Gemma
off Don's shoulders and heads back to the bedroom with her.

PANEL: DON'S SELF-LOATHING SCAMPERS UP HIS PANT LEG. DON TRIES TO
SHAKE IT OFF. DON'S BALLOON: WHAT DO YOU WANT? SELF-LOATHING'S
BALLOON: LOSER!

Don starts on the dishes, which he apparently should have
done earlier.

PANEL: DON TRYING TO DROWN HIS SELF-LOATHING IN THE SINK WITH ALL
THE DIRTY DISHES. SELF-LOATHING'S BALLOON: FAGGOT! CHEESE-FACE!

He keeps an eye out the cracked and taped window, on the
field, the grass knee-high, bleached almost white. Later in the evening it turns a pinky colour, then a deep charcoal by the time the
highway lights come on and Sandhu's Used Auto Parts' go off. The

circular path in the grass is invisible then, the cars parked behind Blake's trailer gone, Blake alone inside the trailer eating locusts and wild honey. For now, though, he's still walking. The man and the woman in the wheelchair have left. Blake's been on the path since Don woke with Gemma at six this morning, almost twelve hours, or more—who knows when he started. It has to be a record. Occasionally he sips from the water bottle strapped to his belt, but if he stopped for a whiz or a sandwich, Don missed it.

Nat brings Gemma back to the kitchen and hands her off. On the baby's face, a sated, vaguely drunken expression.

PANEL: GEMMA THE TALKING BABY GLOATS IN DON'S ARMS. HICCUPPING AND SLURRING IN HER BALLOON: DEE-LISHUS! YUMMY, YUMMY! YOU SHOULD TRY IT, POPS!

This is the only time Don feels anything but selfless adoration for his daughter.

From the fridge, Nat takes a foil-wrapped roast chicken she must have picked up on the way home. She drops it on a wet plate.

How was your day? he asks.

Shitty. She disappears inside the fridge again, comes up with an unhappy lettuce. All that way and my contact didn't show. Now I have to make something up.

I'm sorry, says Don.

She tears leaves off and drops them in the salad spinner. Why? It's not your fault.

But it is his fault. She wanted to be the one home with Gemma.

I'm going to talk to your friend, she says.

He's not my friend, Don tells her.

What is not Don's fault is this house. Nat was nesting. Nat insisted they buy, but unless they were prepared never to go on a trip, or even to a restaurant, ever again in their entire lives, they had to buy in the 'burbs. Not Surrey, Don told her. Please. But the realtor found this old farmhouse. Country life awaited them between the highway and a car parts salvage. All they had to do was plant some trees. The trunk of each of these trees is presently the circumference of Don's thumb, but give them twenty years and Sandhu's extensive inventory will eventually be screened.

Less than a month after they moved in, there was a knock at the door. Don answered. Nat was sleeping with Gemma, only a week old.

Picasso? Hey! I can't believe this!

Instantly, Don was doused in sweat. To this day he hasn't bought anything in Surrey, not even gas, because he's afraid of it happening again, of running into someone he went to high school with and his flight instinct not kicking in. However much Don has changed, they'll recognize him.

Blake Alderson, said Blake Alderson, fully justifying Don's paranoia. He held out his hand for Don to shake. Don took it. He had to. Because of that day behind the school, Blake Alderson and Dean Sawitsky with the sticks and the dog shit.

Blake explained about the trailer and needing a big lot. Don was hardly listening. He was thinking how this must happen all the time in places like South Africa and Argentina. Waiting for the bus, shopping in the grocery store, there he is! Your former torturer.

No parties, I promise, said Blake.

He looked sixty years old, Don realized, though he couldn't have been more than a year or two older than Don. Instead of a face, a skull in a leather bag.

No drugs or booze. I'm different. I found Christ.

Don was different too, of course. He'd found Art.


After supper, Don stands at the kitchen window again watching Nat wend her way down to the bottom of the property. Daunting, the sight of her at the fence, rigid with disapproval, hands parked on hips. Any husband would cower. But Blake doesn't alter his pace. Blake is not afraid of Nat. Because the path passes near the fence, it looks as though he's veering across the field, heading directly and purposely for her.

The prodromal signals: sweat, a tightening in his chest, shortness of breath. Gemma in the Jolly Jumper shrieks for attention, but Don can't take his eyes off the window. Blake is just metres away from Nat now and getting closer. He's almost at the fence. There. He's right in front of her, partially eclipsed by Nat.

Nat turns her head, watches him pass.

Nothing happens.

Don's whole body is tremoring.

PANEL: STRUNG UP IN THE DOORWAY, GEMMA THE TALKING BABY PIROU-ETTES AND SHRIEKS, SPRAYING DROOL. GEM'S BALLOON: GET ME A GRAVOL, QUICK! DON RUSHES TO EXTRICATE HER FROM THE HARNESS WITH SELF-LOATHING ON HIS SHOULDER MAKING FACES AT THE BABY.

He totes Gemma off for her bath. It's all right, he says, still panting. Everything's going to be fine.

Gemma bathes in a ring that keeps her upright and suction-cupped to the bottom of the tub. Still, he can't leave her and go to the window. You can't leave a baby in the bath. He submerges the plastic teapot, tries to get her to fill his cup. He squeaks her duck. All the while he's listening for Nat to come back in, fretting over why she's taking so long. Is she mad enough to go over the fence?

PANEL: DON'S SELF-LOATHING DOING THE BACKSTROKE IN THE TUB. IT RUNS INTO DUCKIE. SELF-LOATHING'S BALLOON: OUT OF THE WAY, YA PIECE OF RUBBER!

When he can stand it no longer, he lifts Gemma out, wraps her in a towel and carries her to the kitchen window. Blake is on the outward swing of the path, walking away from the fence, Nat just then heading back up to the house, head lowered, dark hair concealing her face. Don reads the disappointment in her posture— disappointment in him, in how everything has turned out.

When she comes back inside, she takes Gemma off to bed without a word. Assuming that's the last he'll see of Nat tonight, Don goes dutifully to the living room to tape a crooked seam in the drywall. They are two bookish people trying to fix up an old house using a book. It should be funny. It should be filling every panel of his strip, which is essentially the autobiography of a dweeb, Don, barely muddling through the day. For a long time Don hasn't been able to get the pictures out of his head.

Nat does come back. She comes and lies on the couch and watches him, which makes the tape stick to his fingers.

PANEL: A SINISTER-LOOKING DON ROLLING HIS SELF-LOATHING IN DRY-WALL TAPE. SELF-LOATHING'S BALLOON: UNHAND ME!

She's avoiding writing. Don is familiar with her strategies. The only way she can start is to put it off and put it off until she can scratch her backside on the deadline.

She says, He wouldn't answer.

I could have told you that. You can call him till the ghosts of the cows come home.

Does he ever stop?

He hasn't today.

You'd think he'd want to take a load off. On the Sunshine Coast, people leave their old chairs at the bus stops. Isn't that nice?

Yes. It is.

It drives me crazy watching them. Around and around and around. Because that's what I feel like, driving into work an hour each way, writing about topiaries and sunscreen and sangria. Coming home to the endless Work-In-Progress. I'd just like to hire someone to fix up this dump. I'd like him to pay us so we can hire someone. Is that so unreasonable?

Don says, No.

This should be the happiest time of our lives.

I know, says Don.

Who is he? He looks like some crazy freak.

A guy I went to school with.

You said that already.

Don has hinted things to Nat. Once, for example, he brought up his scars. He said, I can't set foot on a golf course. Men in spiked shoes run after me with clubs trying to get a whack at my face. Nat said, So you had zits. Who didn't?

PANEL: LITTLE DONNY BUTLER RUNNING THE GAUNTLET BETWEEN CLASSES AT SIR JOHNNY MAC. SO MUCH ACNE, HE LOOKS LIKE A SMALLPOX VICTIM. SKOOL-MATES HURL FOOD AND TAUNTS WHICH HE DEFLECTS WITH A FOOD-SPATTERED BINDER.

PANEL: DONNY TAKING REFUGE IN THE ART ROOM. FINGERS CLAW UNDER THE DOOR, TRYING TO GET AT HIM. MRS. LONG IS BUSY AT THE BACK OF THE ROOM RECONSTRUCTING THE VENUS DE MILO OUT OF TAMPAX TUBES. MRS. LONG'S BALLOON: DONNY! COME HERE AND TELL ME WHAT YOU THINK OF THIS.

PANEL: DONNY CROSS-EYED WITH EMBARRASSMENT BEFORE THE SCULPTURE, STEAM POURING FROM HIS EARS. MRS. LONG'S BALLOON: . . . AN AESTHETIC REBUTTAL OF HISTORICALLY MISOGYNISTIC REPRESENTATIONS OF THE FEMALE FORM—OH, HERE'S SOMEONE I WANT YOU TO MEET.

PANEL: GIRL IN BIG GLASSES COMING IN THE DOOR, HOLDING HER NOSE. GIRL'S BALLOON: HI, DONNY. I'M WITH THE YEARBOOK COMMITTEE. MRS. LONG, AH, WE, AH, WE WERE WONDERING IF YOU'D DO PORTRAITS OF THE CLASS OF '79.

PANEL: HEADING: AND SUDDENLY LITTLE DONNY BUTLER'S LIFE TOOK A TURN FOR THE BETTER! DONNY IN THE ART ROOM SKETCHING A BLOW-UP DOLL OF A GIRL. BEHIND HER, ALL THE SKOOL-MATES WHO WERE ABUSING HIM STAND EAGERLY IN LINE.

PANEL: HEADING: BUT ONLY SOME OF THE TIME! DONNY STANDING AT HIS LOCKER. SCRAWLED ACROSS IT: FAGGOT! CHEESE-FACE! I EAT SHIT! DONNY SNIFFS. DONNY'S BALLOON: WHAT'S THAT SMELL?

PANEL: HEADING: THE NEXT DAY. BLAKE ALDERSON STALKING THE HALL. WAIST-LENGTH HAIR, TOOLED LEATHER WRISTBANDS, SLEEVES RIPPED OFF. DONNY SHRINKS DOWN AT HIS LOCKER. DONNY'S BALLOON: OH, NO! THERE'S BLAKE ALDERSON! HE'S PROBABLY THE ONE WHO PUT DOG SHIT IN MY LOCKER YESTERDAY!

PANEL: DONNY TRIES TO SQUEEZE INSIDE THE LOCKER. BLAKE ALDERSON'S BALLOON: HEY, DONNY! I'M TALKING TO YOU.

PANEL: DONNY LOOKS UP, DON'T DO IT! WRITTEN ON HIS FACE. A FEW OF HIS ZITS SPONTANEOUSLY POP, SPLATTERING BLAKE. BLAKE ALDERSON'S BAL-LOON: I FUCKIN' LOVE THAT PICTURE YOU DREW OF ME! CAN YOU DRAW ANOTHER ONE? MAKE IT BIGGER. AND MAKE IT A JOINT, NOT A CIGARETTE.

PANEL: BLAKE HOLDS UP THE PICTURE OF HIMSELF, GRINNING. BLAKE'S BAL-LOON: THIS IS FUCKIN' GREAT! I CAN'T BELIEVE YOU DID IT JUST LIKE THAT! I'M PUTTING IT ON THE FRIDGE, MAN.

Don tells Nat, Once I was leaving school late. He assumes she won't understand that this meant no witnesses, that he could be singled out at a glance. I was drawing pictures for the yearbook. Caricatures of the graduating class.

It was likely Mrs. Long, the art teacher, who got the yearbook committee to ask him. Years later, at the time of the Columbine massacre, Don wondered about the art teacher because Mrs. Long was the only one he would have spared had he a taste for revenge, which he doesn't. Because of the yearbook gig, Don had to stay after school a few times a week, drawing. People who'd never spoken to him in his life, even people who unfortunately had, began sucking up. They wanted bigger boobs, smaller noses, braces and pimples left out. Suddenly Little Donny Butler possessed the transforming powers of a god.

Giving up with the drywall tape, Don moves to the chair across from where Nat lies and puts his feet up on the tool box. At the back of the gym, he tells her, there was an emergency exit with an overhang where the smokers sometimes hung out. I was going home that way and I saw Blake Alderson and Dean Sawitsky there.

PANEL: BLAKE AND DEAN, SLEEVELESS. SCRIBBLED HAIR, TOOLED LEATHER.
HEADING: NOTE THE SUPERB LATERAL VISION POSSESSED BY PREDATORS.

I saw them. Blake and Dean. But I had to keep going. If I turned back or if I ran, they'd come after me. If I kept walking they might just call me names.

What names? Nat asks.

Don tells her one of the more benign ones, Cheese-face, and Nat laughs.

Nat laughs!

Anyway, he says, I kept on walking and they didn't notice me. I took this as a ruse. I lived this scenario so often it was like chess. As I got nearer, I saw they were leaning over something. They were bending over something and laughing. They had sticks. They'd caught something and were torturing it with sticks.

Nat rises on an elbow and looks at him.

I didn't want to see what it was, says Don.

What was it?

Some kind of animal, I thought. I hoped it was dead.

What? Nat asks.

It was a pile of dog shit. They were playing with it. They had it sort of pincushioned with sticks.

The black spiky mound appears in every one of his cartoons. He has several dozen sketchbooks filled only with this image.

Once they put shit in his locker, but the janitor cleaned it up. Don would have rather they just pounded him. Anything but what he thought they were going to do. He tried his usual useless last resort, negotiating with the deity, please God, please, though he didn't believe in God anymore. Don't let them make me. Please. By then Blake and Dean were behind him, leaving Don in the worst possible tactical position. He could never outrun them. Looking over his shoulder to see if they were following—that was their signal. One backward glance and—go!

He thought, I'll kill myself. If one molecule of that shit so much as touches me.

PANEL: BLAKE AND DEAN BENDING OVER THE MOUND. DON'S SELF-LOATHING LEAPS TO ITS FEET AND RUNS. BLAKE AND DEAN'S BALLOON: HEY! WHAT'S GOING ON? COME BACK! FAR IN THE BACKGROUND, DONNY STALKS AWAY WITH A NOOSE DANGLING OVER HIS HEAD.

I had a hard time, Don tells Nat. All the way through school. It was hell.

PANEL: DONNY IN HIS BASEMENT AT HOME, STANDING ON A CHAIR, A ROPE COLLARING HIS NECK. HE'S TYING THE END TO A RAFTER. SELF-LOATHING WATCHES. SELF-LOATHING'S BALLOON: HEY! WHAT DO YOU THINK YOU'RE DOING?

PANEL: DONNY LOOKS DOWN AT THE SPIKY BLACK CREATURE. DONNY'S BAL-LOON: WHERE'D YOU COME FROM? SELF-LOATHING'S BALLOON: YOU'RE NOT GOING TO GET OFF SO EASY! COME DOWN RIGHT NOW!

Nat says, What happened?

And all Don can bring himself to tell her is this: Blake said hi.

He said hi?

He called me Picasso. When I walked by, that's what he said. Hi, Picasso.

Don goes to the kitchen to get a drink of water, lifts the glass with a shaking hand. Outside, every highway light is haloed. There's another light too, smaller and closer, not stationary, but moving slowly in an arc. Blake Alderson, walking around by flashlight.

Don sets the glass in the sink and leaves by the kitchen door. There are no stairs, which is why they don't normally go out this way. Don has to jump into a void. He closes the door then stands for a long time watching the drunken firefly that is Blake's light, wondering once again what he should do and feel about the man. It's true that after Don drew the picture of Blake, Blake never bothered him again. Not that day behind the school. Never again. But what about everything that happened before that? Don should just forgive and forget? Or should he thank Blake? Thank you, Blake, because, without you and your ilk, I would not be the syndicated dweeb I am today.

Above his head the kitchen window slides open and Nat calls his name.

Nat sees Blake too, she must. For a long time they watch him, Don just under the window, so close to Nat that if he reached up and Nat out, their hands would touch. In actual fact, they've never been so far apart.

Don? Are you out there?

Eventually the window slams.

After a minute, when he's sure Nat has left the kitchen, Don walks down to the bottom of the lot. There's a moon to see by, silvering the way. He leans against the fence watching Blake on the slow homeward swing now, the flashlight beam sweeping the path as he advances. Don hasn't been standing very long when he begins wishing for a chair.

Blake passes in the dark, a shadow of himself. Fuck you, Don says. Blake staggers on without responding so Don climbs the fence and waits for him to come around again. He's walking so slowly, it takes him almost ten minutes to complete the circuit, by which time Don's ass is numb and he has no choice but to get off the fence. He jumps down on Blake's side.

Fucker.

He wades through the grass to the tamped-hard path, falls into step. Asshole.

PANEL: BLAKE ALDERSON, SEMI-CONSCIOUS, DRAGGING HIMSELF AROUND THE CIRCLE, DON FOLLOWING. DON'S BALLOON: ASSHOLE! SHITHEAD! STONER!

Each of these insults Don pronounces in a low clear voice. He'd scream them, but then Nat would come out. Tailing Blake in the dark, feeling his way with his feet, thinking of the most outrageous, puerile things, then saying them. Shit licker. Toilet-paper face. Cum wad. Christ! Where is this coming from? Don almost stumbles but recovers his footing and continues pelting these ludicrous expletives at the silhouette of Blake's stooped back. Booger eater. Cock breath. Pus sucker. Bum boil. He feels like an idiot. Then he starts to laugh. It would be funny in the strip, hilarious, but they wouldn't print it.

Shut up, Don thinks. Just shut up.

It's quiet now, hardly any cars on the highway at this hour. No sound but breathing—Blake's ragged, Don's decelerating. And whoa! Down he goes! Blake sinks to his knees like a beast, like the silence has felled him, and Don almost trips over his swaying genuflection. He steps back as Blake thuds onto his side in the long grass.

PANEL: DON'S SELF-LOATHING SPRINGS ONTO BLAKE'S NECK, SCRATCHING AND CHEWING. SELF-LOATHING'S BALLOON: EI-YAH! BLOOD AND SHREDDED THROAT FLESH FLY IN ALL DIRECTIONS.

Blake, fetal and panting. The dropped flashlight shines into the thick of the grass. Don could kick him. If he wanted.

The quiet. The quiet. The quiet.

PANEL: DON CLAPS HIS HANDS. DON'S BALLOON: OKAY! ENOUGH! SCAT! HIS SELF-LOATHING SKEEDADDLES, GLARING OVER ITS SPINY SHOULDER.

Probably a rat. A scurrying in the grass. Something humps off. Don sees it in the beam of light.

Neither of them speaks for several minutes.

# The Maternity Suite

## The Reluctant Grandmother

By dinner Betty was desperate, nerves bunched together like in that carnival game where you tug one of the hundred gathered strings to see what prize jumps. In this case, she was her own twitchy, jerky prize. She tossed the shrimp in the cream sauce then spooned it over the pasta butterflies. The pepper mill, cranked, made the same sound as her teeth.

Carey tucked in the moment Betty set his plate down. Anna only winced. "Ma," she said. "I can't eat this."

"Why not?" Betty snapped.

"Because. Because—"

Betty was about to leave right then, stalk off in a fury and light up—to hell with them!—except that Carey beat her to it. He lurched from the table and bolted out of the room. Down the hall the bathroom door slammed, but they could still hear his toilet-amplified retching. She turned to Anna. "What's the matter with Carey?"

"I'm going to have a baby!"

Instinctively, Betty pressed her hands to her own slack belly, a maternal salute. Eighteen months before, Pauline, her other daughter, had shown up unannounced after a year away in Mexico.

When Betty opened the front door her uterus, completely docile since menopause, suddenly contracted. Yet it had taken her another full second to recognize Pauline on the step, tanned and eight months pregnant. Betty didn't like to think a reproductive organ might have an intelligence of its own.

"Anna," she said, tenderly she hoped. "How far along are you?"

"About eight weeks." Anna put her face in her hands and began to sob.

"What? What's wrong?"

"Nothing. I'm happy. I can't stop crying, that's all. I cry all day long."

"That's normal." She meant hormones, though Anna had always been sentimental and easy to bring to tears. She took Anna's plate to the counter and scraped the pasta back into the pot, realizing then that the shrimp was what must have put Anna off. The clump of cells inside her would be about that colour, size and shape.

Carey reappeared, still looking queasy. "I told her," said Anna, holding out her hand to him. He glanced at Betty, turned bright crimson, looked away. Guilty, Betty thought, and laughed out loud. *Nowadays they actually feel guilty for what they do to us.*

"He didn't know it would be like this," said Anna.

"Like what?"

"Sick-making," said Carey. "All my life if someone throws up, I throw up. I don't know how much more I can take."

"It's normal," Betty said again. She put a consoling arm around him, her favourite son-in-law—her only one.

Two years before, Betty's husband, Robert, had rejoined the flock. Thursday afternoons the little Reverend would arrive looking every inch his denomination in corduroys and earnestness. He met Robert in his room, the one that used to be the den when Robert could climb stairs, actually got him out of bed and cross-legged on the floor seemingly by murmuring appeasements to his pain.

The Light of Christ was a radiant presence in the room, Betty had learned listening outside the door. "Inhale. With every breath you are filled with Healing Light." She brought in tea and Robert's medication on a tray, marvelling because the little Reverend was so gay. During the height of the ordination controversy, Robert had referred to the United Church as "The Church of the Perverts."

At least the Reverend could take credit for making a better smoker out of Betty. Standing on the patio after Anna and Carey had gone home, she inhaled with fervour, paused ecstatically, then blew a pillar of smoke above her head, all the way to heaven. A mid-July evening, warm, the garden climaxing in tufts and pouches, cups, bells, horns, spires, bristles, balls, stars. She unwound and turned on the hose, aiming the sprinkling nozzle low at the impatiens in the shaded bed along the fence. Her children forbade her to smoke. Cancer had mouldered away their father and now they began their visits with an inspection of her home, sniffing room to room, checking potted plants for butts, not letting her out of sight. Today Anna had found a disposable lighter in the liquor cabinet and, with a shriek, had thrown it on the living-room carpet. The very sight of the gaudy blue cylinder set off a Pavlovian response in Betty, her cravings worsening through the afternoon until nicotine stained everything, even Anna's happy news. So crabbed by the time Anna blurted her announcement, Betty's first thought had been a sour wondering what Carey and Anna would raise a child on. Anna had never finished her degree. Carey languished on some substitute list and when he taught, it was only English to refugees. How lucrative could that be?

Water pooled around the impatiens drooping from the day's heat. Soon they would perk as Betty, her cigarette half smoked, was perking now. She tugged on the hose, raised and swung the nozzle around to the sunny wall of the house. The water, soaring above her in a parabola, caught the light and for a dazzling, prismatic moment became a sheen of rainbow against the white stucco wall. Mist hit her, pinging cold against her face and arms. Then a feeling, too, showered down, a tingling.

Joy for her daughter, at last.

The phone rang after midnight. Betty answered to a hiss: "You're smoking, aren't you?" Then Pauline's real voice asked, "Did Anna tell you?"

"Yes."

"She just wants a baby because I have Rebecca. She always has to have what I have."

"That's unkind," Betty chided, though the very thought had crossed her own mind earlier, before she'd had that cigarette. She could hear the supposedly coveted Rebecca in the background, Rebecca or a siren, and wondered if Pauline ever put the child to bed or just let her cry herself to sleep behind the television.

Pauline was really calling, she said, to tell Betty about the dream she'd had the night before. "Me and Anna went to visit you in the hospital because you'd had a baby. Except when we got there, we found out you'd actually had a cat. The weird thing was the cat didn't surprise us at all. We just wondered why it was full grown and not a kitten. Different gestation periods I guess. Nine months is probably way more time than you need for a kitten. Do you think I dreamed it because of Smitty?"

Smitty was Pauline's grey and black six-toed tabby, a biter. Since Rebecca had started walking, Smitty had begun stalking. Betty had advised neutering. The world, in Betty's opinion, would be a better place if everyone were neutered. "Have you taken him to the vet yet?" she asked.

"How's this for a coincidence? The same day Anna announces she's knocked up, Smitty gets his balls chopped off!"

Laughing, Betty said good night and hung up. She stared for a moment at the still-life arrangement on the bedside table: *Nature morte avec téléphone et fruits.* Anna had put the fruit bowl there so

Betty could nibble away her late night cravings. Fruit of my womb, she thought, holding up a waxy red apple. In her other hand she held an orange.

Pauline was born tangled in umbilical cord and with her first shrill and indignant vocalization seemed to announce that she would never be tied up or down again. Then, as if anyone could have mistaken her meaning, she continued screaming for three months. It was a demand for love fiercer than Betty had ever imagined. Her nipples cracked from giving and Pauline drew her blood.

Anna was the quiet one, so placid she was cast as the Infant Jesus in the United Church nativity play where previously they had used a big bald doll. Pauline, three years old that Christmas, flossy in her lamb's suit, clustered with the rest of the preschool flock around Anna in the manger. Betty and Robert could hear her crying "Meow," while everyone else bleated. At home after the service, Pauline insisted Anna be put to bed in a box in the garage.

In later years, Anna graduated to playing Mary. Pauline had no further interest in Sunday school theatrics; the days and nights of her real life provided drama enough. Her preteen vocational aspiration was to be a bank robber. She shoplifted for practice and got caught. Robert, in charge of discipline, of disciplining Pauline, grounded her for a year. This didn't stop the boys from coming. So skinny, shaggy and sullen, all wearing the same grey hooded sweatshirts as they filed down to the rumpus room, they reminded Betty of a chain gang. She strongly suspected Pauline had relinquished her virginity at thirteen, probably in their own basement, though she could never bring herself to ask. Whom could she blame for her daughter's loss? She and Robert were decent people. They had faults, certainly; they played too much bridge, for example, but they had never modelled lust.

She remembered Pauline showing her an advertisement in *Teen*. "What's Tampax?" She was only ten at the time, too young, Betty thought, to know how tedious her fate would be. "I wish," Betty had answered, "you wouldn't read those magazines."

So perhaps her own prudishness had contributed to Pauline's preternatural curiosity. She vowed to do better by Anna. "Inside a woman's body is a nest," she told her, and from Anna's perplexed look Betty knew she was thinking of twigs and grass and tangled bits of string.

"It's made of blood."

Anna's bottom lip began to quiver. "I know! Pauline told me, but I hoped it wasn't true!"

Anna being prettier than Pauline, taller and fair, Betty had expected from her an even longer line of convict suitors. They never came. On Friday nights Anna went to the library with her girlfriends. She joined a swim club and spent every weekend at the pool or painting watercolour pictures of butterflies and flowers in her room. Into adolescence she sailed on gentle breezes. When she was fourteen, she woke up screaming.

Robert drove. Betty sat in the back seat with Anna's head, damp with sweat, cradled in her lap, Anna moaning and panting and clutching her abdomen.

In a curtained-off corner of the emergency room, Betty helped a nurse strip Anna and get her into the flimsy gown. She hadn't meant to look at her daughter's naked body, but glimpsed, in spite of herself, pubic hair and a white tympanum of belly, round and taut. The doctor, when he finally appeared, kneaded Anna pitilessly where her pain was. "How old are you?" he asked and when Anna answered through gritted teeth, he glanced at Betty. "Could she be pregnant?"

Anna wailed.

"Now, now," he said. "These things happen. Let me have a look."

It was what Betty had always feared, of course, but from Pauline. Her ashamed face in her hands, she heard their bustling preparations: the snap of a rubber glove, a scraping chair, then an odd

"Oh!" from the doctor, repeated by the whispered-to nurse. She looked up to see Anna's feet in the stirrups. The doctor had vanished. The nurse, smiling, said, "Don't worry. She'll be fine," and hurried out leaving Betty alone with Anna. If only Robert were here, Betty thought, though she was also relieved he wasn't. It was a female crisis. His proper place was behind the steering wheel, and now in the waiting room; Robert instinctively understood this. Still, she could have used him to raise Cain with the staff.

Leaning over Anna, Betty asked her coldly, "Who did this to you?" but Anna only whimpered and shook her head. Betty recalled an article in one of Pauline's magazines. It usually happened to skinny girls like Anna, or girls disguised by fat—either way, it didn't show—girls, good and confused, who had no idea what sex was. Had some boy asked her to close her eyes, insisting it was his finger? Or worse, some grown-up lech? A teacher?

"You should tell me things!"

"What things?" Anna sobbed.

Suddenly the narrow space at the end of the bed accommodated a crowd—the nurse and doctor, interns, and Dr. So-and-so, barely introduced, from Ob-Gyn. They opened Anna's legs like a textbook and immediately began to thrill. The gynecologist said something about a "membrane" and someone else pointed out the "bulge." These words together offended Betty, as did the faces gaping, via the speculum, in her daughter's deepest, most private place. Behind the curtains like this, she was reminded of a freak-show tent or a travelling brothel in the desert. She jerked the sheet down over Anna's spread legs.

"What is going on?"

It was the farthest thing from a baby. Rare, but not serious: an imperforated hymen. Menstrual blood had been accumulating inside Anna for months.

Betty walked beside the stretcher as it coursed the antiseptic halls. No one could be purer than Anna, she was thinking. They could operate, puncture her with their instruments, but never penetrate her innocence. This was the kind of romantic nonsense she could entertain during a crisis. Afterward, she wouldn't even remember thinking it.

At the end of her first trimester Anna asked Betty to come and help her paint the room that would be the nursery. No more than a glorified closet, up to now it had been their study. Betty took the pictures off the walls. They folded up the trestle desk, moved it and the blue plastic Ikea chair into the bedroom, then set to clearing the bookshelves of the pregnancy guides and all the texts that were the evidence of Anna's flighty university career: psychology, anthropology, art history. Lugging an armload into the bedroom, Betty paused to read the title on the first huge volume and wondered how anyone could be so wordy on the irrelevant subject of Flemish painting.

In the tiny kitchen she made tea. Anna staggered through, a tower of books in her arms, strands of blond hair escaping from her ponytail—glowing, Betty had to admit. She looked like the Madonna on the cover of the textbook. "You'd better be careful," she warned. "Let's take a break."

"How did you feel when you were pregnant with me, Ma?"

Betty passed her a mug of tea. "I don't remember."

"How can you not remember?"

"We didn't make a fuss like you."

"Who's making a fuss?"

"You and Pauline. Back then you'd be as big as a house and no one would pass comment."

"Daddy wasn't with you, I guess."

"In the delivery room?" Betty snorted. "Certainly not. The only good thing about men in delivery rooms is a declining birth rate."

"Oh, Ma!"

Overpopulation had been one of Betty and Robert's "topics." On this very subject they'd spent many a pleasurable evening agreeing with each other in outraged tones. Betty told Anna, "Only in developed countries is the birth rate dropping. Only in developed countries are men looking where they shouldn't. Why would you want Carey to see you like that?"

"It's beautiful."

"Ach!" Betty set down her mug, exasperated. All Pauline and Anna talked about now, lounging in Betty's backyard and sipping endless blender drinks, was the glory of nausea and stretch marks. Rebecca, meanwhile, the product of Pauline's nine months of masochistic indulgence, toddled unsupervised through the flower beds eating dirt. What Betty was thankful for at least: they finally had something in common. It used to be that whenever they got near one another, Pauline would drop a rose and run. If Anna so much as looked the wrong way at Pauline, Pauline would fly at her shrieking "Noogie!" and grate her knuckles mercilessly across Anna's skull. This, even after they had both finished high school and ought to have been comporting themselves like adults. Now, finally, after all these years, they seemed like sisters.

Anna asked, accusing, "Did you smoke?"

"Yes, I smoked. Nobody told us not to."

"I might have been damaged, you know."

"Well, you weren't." Betty drained her mug and stood. "Okay. Let's paint."

In the little room, Anna knelt to pry open one of the cans with a screwdriver.

"Is Carey working today?" Betty asked.

"I don't know."

"Why isn't he helping?"

"He's not very useful," said Anna with a sigh.

Why marry then, thought Betty, if not to have a live-in painter, plumber and small appliance repairman? But she didn't say it; a blade had appeared on her tongue the second Anna mentioned smoking. She did love Carey, just not as much as cigarettes.

The lid popped off the can. "Is that the colour you want?" asked Betty, dubious.

Anna stirred the paint then tipped the can and let it pour, a rich, warm stream, into the rolling tray. "I think it's going to be a girl."

Betty said, "I'd call that red."

That night she went through the photo albums but could only find one picture of herself pregnant. Black-and-white, it showed her and Pauline hand in hand against a backdrop of shadowy trees, her body half turned away from Pauline, face to the camera. Visible in profile under her cotton sundress was the bulge of Anna. Where had she got that dress? She couldn't remember ever being so feminine. Burly, energetic, she had spent most of her youth in trousers, like a girl in one of those old Workers' Party posters with a pole over her shoulder and a huge red flag unfurling behind.

With Pauline she squabbled endlessly over feminism. According to Pauline, every problem a woman faced was the fault of men. Her own hypocritical consorting with the oppressor she rationalized away with semantics. Pauline did not say "men"; she said "the patriarchy." Naturally, no one epitomized the patriarchy for Pauline more than poor Robert, who was only fulfilling his responsibilities. Betty felt sorry for men today, she really did. How confused they must be!

"Bladder infections," Pauline gave as an example. Busy tending selflessly to the needs of others, women neglected to take the time to void.

"What rubbish!" Betty had crowed. "Have you ever heard of self-control?"

Evidently not, for Pauline couldn't even name the culprit who had knocked her up in Mexico. Betty, though, was of that stalwart generation that could hold its urine all day if it had to. If hunger needled her, she looked at her watch, decided when to eat and felt not a pang until that time. Even when Robert had crept across the ravine of decency that separated their twin beds, she never let go of the reins of her senses. She focused instead on the ingredients and steps for making bouillabaisse.

But at times in her life the flag behind her had changed from red to white—an unconditional surrender—in pregnancy and, later, when menopause vanquished her, just as cancer had Robert. With the little Reverend at his side, Robert had battled against his dying body, but his body had won. Now that he was gone, Betty carried on the struggle, faced the same surly foe, clad now not in the armour of disease but craving. She couldn't even lay out a game of solitaire without a fight.

She closed the photo album, returned it to the shelf, left the den and climbed the stairs. Undressing for bed, she paused before the dresser mirror with her nightgown in her hand. The enemy's other guise was age. Her breasts had flattened, skin sagged all over like a too-large garment.

"We are a will," she said out loud, "dressed up in a body."

The telephone rang. Naked, Betty crossed over to the bedside table where two red apples softened in the bowl. On the third ring, she slid her fingers under the phone and drew out the cigarette. The phone shrilled, a proxy. Ignoring it, she wandered the room, cigarette defiantly between her lips. She was searching, searching for the lighter she'd hidden.

## The Expectant Mother

The professor was explaining something marvellous a little monk had done with sweet peas. Anna closed her eyes and pictured the flowers that scaled the fence in their yard every summer, a tangle of moth-winged blooms, some pink, others red or mauve or white. As a girl she believed Jesus made dawn rounds through the garden with a brush and palette, mixing paints with dew. Now, at twenty, that was the explanation she still preferred. Science was not saving her father. All it had done was disillusion her.

Someone poked her with a pencil. Starting, she turned to face the smirk of the person sitting next to her. He had a long neck prominently knobbed with an Adam's apple and straight hair parted down the middle, neither blond nor brown but some sheenless shade between. "When it comes to genes," he said, "Levi Strauss is still the man for me."

"My father has cancer." She began to cry and Carey to panic—something that would happen again and again until they were married, and after too.

"Do you want to talk?" he asked her. "Do you want to get out of here? Hey, let's get out of here." He stuffed his notebook into his army satchel and took her by the hand. Tripping and premature, their exit. The professor at the front of the hall droned on. Probably he was thinking his words were having no effect, but he was wrong, for instead of a veil she'd worn a wreath of sweet peas on her head. They were married in her parents' backyard just weeks before her father died. Reverend Chalmer performed the ceremony, her father's wish, not Anna's. Also present were Carey's mother from Nova Scotia, who turned out to be as awful as Carey had claimed, and a few of Anna's high school friends. Pauline was in Mexico living loosely under the sun.

The reception afterward was at The Teahouse. "If only that woman weren't so morose," Betty had told Anna in the washroom as they reapplied their lipstick. She meant Carey's mother. "You'd think she was paying."

"If only Pauline had come," said Anna, solely to remind her mother of the slight.

"That too."

"If only Daddy would get better!"

"Stop it," said Betty.

Her father hadn't been able to give her away properly, but had waited in a wheelchair by the birdbath while Anna had walked the green aisle of the lawn alone. When he took her hand and squeezed, it was with the last of his strength.

"I wish we'd had a different minister."

"Enough!" Betty shooed Anna out of the washroom, staying behind a few minutes herself—to smoke. Anna wasn't fooled.

During pre-nuptial counselling Reverend Chalmer had seemed to suggest they shouldn't marry. First, he'd insinuated that student loans would undo them. Couldn't they wait until they'd finished school and were more financially stable?

"No," was Anna's flat reply.

He talked about maturity. They were only in their early twenties. Did they really know if they were—he searched a long time for the right word—compatible? Anna reddened. What was the Reverend getting at? He wasn't married. What did he know? But in the end, he agreed to unite them, did it with pleasure, seemingly, as if his reservations were the petals that had been tossed as confetti. At dinner he even raised his glass to them. "If you ever have a need, come and see me," Anna overheard him tell Carey.

"God give you love," was his toast.

As soon as Robert died, Anna dropped out of university. A bride of less than a month, it should have been the happiest time of her life, but she couldn't stop crying. She became like one of those mourners for hire, grieving for all concerned: for the stoical Betty, for Carey, who didn't know Robert well enough to care, and for Pauline, who wasn't even there. Carey was very patient with her during these months. When she woke crying in the night he would hold her. He understood her reluctance to begin marital relations, preoccupied as she was with Robert's illness and then his passing. He said it was a relief to him.

Countless times during childhood Anna had envisioned a funeral, but it was always Pauline's. In her imagination, she threw herself on the open casket, on top of Pauline as cold in death as she'd been in life. It wasn't so much Pauline's death that she wished for, as recognition for what she had suffered as her father's favourite. And, of course, relief from Pauline's bully presence, which Mexico had at least provided.

When she heard Pauline was back, though, Anna rushed right over with Carey. She wanted to show Carey to her. Confronted with her sister's condition, Anna was scandalized and Pauline, sensing it, only flaunted her queen-sized self all the more. With her feet up on the coffee table, she commanded them with a fluttering hand: a cup of tea, a hot water bottle, her slippers off. When they were not scurrying back and forth to run her errands, two of them were required to heave her off the couch so she could go to the bathroom. Pauline had pulled a fast one on them all, Anna realized. Automatically she had earned the solicitude of everyone, despite how selfishly she'd behaved. It wasn't fair. Pauline hadn't even apologized for not coming back for the wedding. She hadn't mentioned Robert once.

Then the unexpected happened. After almost two days of labour, Pauline produced nine pounds seven ounces of healthy baby girl. The family reunited around her hospital bed waiting for the nurse to fetch Rebecca, listening to the details of Pauline's ordeal as she wolfed food off the meal tray. She claimed to be stitched from stem to stern. The white of one of her eyes had filled with blood. Pauline happened to glance up from her pudding cup as the nurse wheeled in the bassinet. A besotted smile bloomed on her face. She wouldn't let any of them hold Rebecca. Clutching her tight, cooing feverishly, she consented only to opening the blanket that swaddled her so that they might get a better peek.

"Isn't she a little dear!" cried Betty. Anna almost burst into tears. She thought she'd never seen anything as beautiful as those pursed, petal lips squeezed between pink rounds of cheek.

The next day, when Pauline came home, Anna and Carey went over to help out, as they did almost every day for the next six weeks. Betty was the only one with any experience but, as Carey pointed out, it was almost a quarter century out of date. He took on the job of reading aloud from the manual. Pauline slept between feedings. Betty and Anna, holding the baby in turns, couldn't believe the change in Pauline. It was nothing short of a transformation. If Pauline had turned to stone they would have been less surprised, because stone would have been in character.

Of course, it wasn't just Pauline who had changed. The whole family had been brought together as they never had been before, not even when Robert was dying. Anna, who had always believed in miracles anyway, took this very much to heart.

In the three blocks that she'd walked from the naturopath, every passerby met her eye and smiled. Her hands in her pockets, she could feel the not so secret swell through the lining of her coat. The baby was fully formed inside her now, but only six inches long, its skin transparent, in her imagination radiant, like the little dove in the Van Eyck *Annunciation*.

She crossed the street to the deli. The naturopath had recommended she start massaging her perineum with olive oil, but as she stepped inside, goat bells clanking her entrance, the aroma made her instantly ravenous and she went straight over to the pastry case instead. Belly pressed into the glass, she gazed down at the trays of diamond-cut baklava, the little bales of shredded wheat sopped with honey. A man with a large nose and black Einstein hair came over. "Bea-u-ti-ful la-dy. How can I help you?"

Anna pointed through the glass. "Two pieces."

"Two?" He winked. "For me and for you?"

"For me and my husband."

"Husband?" The knife snatched up, he aimed at his heart, abruptly detouring into the pastry case and, with the tip, sliding the baklava into a paper envelope.

Anna hesitated. "Maybe another for the bus."

He tucked a third piece in. "An even number is better. Why not four?"

"All right." She was just so hungry all the time. Taking the envelope from him, she asked, "Where's your olive oil?"

"Ah! I will take you to the olive grove myself." He came out from behind the counter and swaggered on ahead, apron strings tied in a droopy bow over the empty seat of his pants. Down an aisle of coffee and grape leaves she followed, past red-eyed olives suspended in vinegar and black olives in an open vat. The oil was displayed across three shelves—yellow, gold, amber, green.

"This is best. This is for you." He reached for a small bottle, the deepest of the greens, and placed it in her hands. "This is *extra virgin*."

"What happened to me," Pauline told Anna, "was every time I sneezed, I peed. A line appeared from here to here. The *linea negra*, right? Also, I felt happy. I realized I'd never been happy in all my life."

It didn't occur to Anna to ask the reason for her sister's chronic unhappiness. All she wondered was why she didn't have a line down her own belly like Pauline had had. Before she could ask what exactly it had looked like, Pauline sat up from where she'd been stretched out on the couch licking honey off her fingers. "Where's Rebecca? Rebecca!"

The little girl came teetering around the corner, all pink gums and wide-spaced teeth. Anna didn't like her toddler smile or cob-

web hair, or the ugly red scratches on her arms and face. She'd
been such a perfect baby; it was a pity. Looking elsewhere instead,
Anna noticed the cat. Striped, broad in the paw, it was the reason
Pauline had come over unannounced and eaten the last piece of
baklava, the one Anna was saving for Carey: she was here to dump
it on them. Pupils dilated, fixed blackly on the child, it was inch-
ing forward, low against the carpet.

Uh-oh, Anna thought.

It joggled side to side then darted, reared up and boxed Rebecca
twice. Rebecca stood there stunned. "Smitty!" Pauline screamed,
setting off the child. "Fuck you, Smitty!" She turned accusingly to
Anna. "You see why you've got to take him?"

"But what about when our baby comes?"

"By then Rebecca will be old enough to bash him back. Hush,
baby. Hush." She scooped up the sobbing child and began to bounce
her—roughly, Anna thought.

Anna went to the bedroom, returning a moment later with the
manual. Pauline was trying to wipe Rebecca's face with her sweatshirt sleeve, streaking a slug-trail of mucus along it, Rebecca still
wailing. "Enough!" Pauline thunked her down. Rebecca followed
Pauline back to the couch, frantic arms stretched out. "What do
you want? You want a tittie?" Swinging her onto her knee, she
runched up her sweatshirt; a breast came tumbling out.

"It says here somewhere," said Anna, scanning the index, "that
I should stay away from cats. I could catch something."

"That's only if you mess around with the litter box. Carey can
change the litter box. Where is Carey?"

"He'll be home soon. He got a three-month contract, did I tell
you?" She was searching the columns for *litter box*.

"Do your breasts hurt?" asked Pauline.

Anna looked up. "Did yours?"

"They throbbed."

"They hurt a little," she said, patting herself.

By the time Carey came home, Rebecca had fallen asleep nursing, her wispy head thrown back on Pauline's thigh, air percolating through blocked nostrils. "Ah!" he said when he saw the child. He leaned over her, stage-whispering, "Becky. Little Beck-Beck. Who's your papa? Who's your daddy? It's all right. You can tell me."

Pauline laughed. Carey was allowed to joke like this but when Anna or their mother asked, Pauline flipped. She'd probably slept with a lot of Mexicans—Anna shuddered at the thought—except Rebecca was so colourless, it seemed an unlikely paternity. The little girl looked as if she were kept in a closet half the time.

Carey pressed Rebecca's nose, blinked at his finger and wiped it on his sweater, then went to change out of his teaching clothes. He liked children, Anna knew he did. Even her mother had said he would make a good father. "He's wonderful with Pauline's bastard," were her words.

"Are you staying for supper?" Anna asked Pauline.

In the bedroom, Carey screamed a second before Smitty came tearing out. Pauline got to her feet, Rebecca flopping in her arms. "No," she said. "We better go."

Carey said he didn't know what hit him, or, more precisely, what had seized his Achilles tendon and sunk in its teeth. It was a surprising reaction because usually when Carey was angry he just hunkered down and refused to speak.

"First you spring a baby on me and now this kamikaze cat!"

"Why?" Anna cried in renewed torment. "Why don't you want the baby?"

Carey punched the wall, hard enough that he winced.

"People are starting to wonder!" she told him.

"Wonder *what?*"

"Why you aren't helping!"

"What people?" he screamed.

"Ma! She thought it was strange you weren't there to paint the nursery!"

Carey sneered. "That's not a nursery. That's a room in a bordello."

It was where she ran to, where she always went now when they had a fight. Her back against the wall, she slid down it then collapsed onto her side, sobbing, but with gulping pauses in between so she could hear Carey's approaching steps. After a few minutes she rolled over onto her back, her sobs directed outward instead of muffled by the carpet. Soon she was whimpering instead of crying, but gave that up eventually and just lay there on the floor in the empty room watching the walls pulse all around her.

The door pushed open and Smitty came padding in. Thrumming, he rubbed the whole smooth length of himself across her wet face.

"Carey?" she called, picking fur out of her mouth. "Carey?"

At least he still went with her to their childbirth classes. He enjoyed them because, out of all the husbands, he was the only comedian. During the first class, Judy, the instructor, had passed around a pink plush fetus held by Velcro inside a cloth uterus.

"This is a good model because, like us, it's three-dimensional and soft."

"And in winter," Carey added, "it doubles as a toque!" He tore out the fetus and popped the uterus on his head, cracking up the class.

When a worried woman asked, "What if we lose our baby?" Carey had piped up with the suggestion that she pin her phone number to its diaper. Everyone laughed again. They didn't know how things were at home. They thought he was funny all the time.

Tonight, as Anna lay on the blue vinyl exercise mat to do the breathing exercises, a nervous fluttering began inside her, like small wings beating back and forth. She grabbed Carey's hand.

The room was full of people. He couldn't very well pull away this time.

"There." She pressed his hand to her belly. "Do you feel it?"

From the relaxation tape: surf, plainting gulls, the low murmur of rain, a foghorn's hollow echo. Were there any sadder sounds in the world? The men were all kneeling beside their wives, rubbing the women's temples in the slow and gentle circles Judy had taught. But Carey just stared down at Anna, on his face an indeterminate expression, more than one feeling, none very nice.

When they had put away the mats, Judy said, "Let's talk about sex. After all, that's how you got into this mess in the first place."

Everyone turned to Carey, waiting for the wisecrack.

That night Anna stepped gingerly out of her panties, looked down and knew at once she'd have to start to pray again. She should have started sooner. She hoped it wasn't too late.

This was something nobody knew about, not even her mother or Carey, certainly not Pauline. As a girl she used to build altars, then collect butts from the ashtrays, amassing the stale tobacco threads to burn on them. Sometimes her ceremonies included a live beetle crucified on a pin and slaps she would give herself. Also, she had to refrain from unclean thoughts and picture everything perfect and neat. Before bed each night she would open the bible at random and memorize the line under her finger no matter what little sense it made, which was where she had got the notion of thoughts being clean or unclean in the first place. If she did all these things, then her prayers would be answered. She won two swim meets this way and didn't get warts, despite Pauline holding her down and noogying her infected knuckles all over Anna's face. It was through prayer, too, that she had been able to delay getting her first period by two years. All the other girls had started by age twelve, but Anna had been fourteen.

She stoppered the drain, turned on the cold water and watched the basin fill. Would it have smoothed things, she wondered, if she'd told all this to Reverend Chalmer? Maybe he would have liked her more if he had known how pious she could be. Looking back, she felt as though he had put a curse on them.

She picked the panties off the floor, bending almost an effort now, and tossed them in the basin. For a minute they floated on the surface of the water until, saturated, their own weight made them sink. White in the white porcelain, soon they settled under the water where the stain loosened and began to lift. It floated slowly upward, a single plume, like red smoke drifting.

## The Suspecting Father

Carey's worst memory was of his mother with a Q-Tip. In dreams his profound dread of it would magnify to her coming at him with a majorette's baton, cotton tipped. For years and years he had stood it. He'd thought it was a ritual that went on in the home of every boy, that after your Sunday night bath your mother would come in and sit on the edge of the tub and, cringing with disgust, clean under your foreskin while you stood shivering on the bath mat. Then he started junior high school, all the naked boys crammed into one big shower stall. He was the only one born in Scotland. Unless you were born in Scotland, he discovered, you didn't even have a foreskin.

He began to lock the door. "Carey?" she would call. "What are you doing in there, Carey?" She probably thought he was abusing himself. She'd always told him, "Carey, never abuse yourself," and he was thrown into confusion. What would she call forcing a cotton swab into the hood of his penis? Hygiene, of course. She'd been a nurse until Carey's father had brought her to Canada. Eventually she let him be, but ever after on a Sunday night she would leave the Q-Tip in a saucer on the vanity.

When the time came for him to go to university, he chose a school as far away as possible from his mother, went from one coast to the other. Every Sunday night she phoned and asked if he was meeting girls, which he was. He wasn't particularly handsome, but what attracted women more than looks, he quickly learned, was a sense of humour, preferably self-deprecating, and a certain wistfulness. He would date them until that first sweet kiss, then abandon them and not return their perplexed calls. His mother never asked if he was keeping himself clean, but that was implied by the very time and day she phoned.

How, then, had he found himself married? Very quickly, it seemed now. Beside him in one of his classes had sat the same extraordinarily beautiful young woman day in and out. She didn't seem to notice him, and at first he thought this was because she was used to being stared at, used to her attention being subtly and not so subtly sought. As the weeks went on, though, he decided she was simply preoccupied. When he finally spoke to her—what a windfall! She actually took him home.

It was to what he saw that afternoon that he let himself be married: an old house filled with plants and brimming ashtrays, half-finished games of solitaire, books, the coffee table stained in interlocking rings from years of G and Ts, radio chattering in the background, crossword puzzles, dust. Outside in her garden Betty, Anna's mother, greeted them with a finger to her lips alongside a dangling cigarette. "Your father's asleep." He was taken into the den to see Robert on a hospital bed, wincing so nobly in his drugged dreams that Carey pictured his own father dying that way, though in reality he'd been killed in a mine accident, instantly, when Carey was an infant. Later a minister visited, just like a vicar in an English novel, and closed himself up with Robert. There was also a sister, he learned, but she was wayward. Wayward. How perfect!

He began to spend part of every day there. No coffee spoons

with the family crest were polished for him. Instead, he was handed a book on composting and the latest issue of *Maclean's* and told to read to Robert until he fell back asleep. Over dinner, Betty expounded her madcap take on world events, French cooking, and how she would try Robert's morphine if she could only be certain she wouldn't end up like some junkie mother in an O'Neill play. Completely sexless was Betty, always in pants, thick waisted with a muscular-looking hump of fat across her back—an ideal woman, Carey thought. He hoped Anna would turn out like that.

Anna was the one who proposed that they marry. She said, "It would mean so much to Daddy and we don't know how much time he has left." Maybe Carey thought he loved her. He certainly felt a surge of something for her when he introduced her to his mother and saw how absolutely she disapproved. At that point, two days before the wedding, he might have changed his mind, but he so badly wanted to defy and disappoint. Of course, in agreeing to marry Anna, it had also occurred to him that wherever he went with her he would be envied by other men, men who were once boys capering in the shower, pointing and laughing at his foreskin.

How quickly everything changed. The old man died, Betty withdrew and Anna's sister reappeared, hugely pregnant. Anna's sister, he had been led to understand, was quite a piece of work. What the hell was Anna then? Carey was soon to wonder.

Though Anna spent most of her time at her mother's anyway, he tried to be home as little as possible. Happily inexperienced as a teacher, it took him hours to prepare his lessons. Afterward, he would go for coffee and read the paper at leisure and sometimes take in a movie too.

He was settling at a window table with the classified section when someone said hello. A man neatly dressed in a jacket and cords. At first Carey didn't recognize, not without the collar, the man ultimately responsible for fucking up his life.

"And a hearty congratulations. I heard your news." The Reverend switched the hand that held his paper cup, extending the right. When Carey took it, it felt small and exceedingly warm.

"May I join you?"

Carey hastened to make room on the tiny tabletop even as he screamed *No, no, no* in his head. The Reverend set down his coffee and, taking off his jacket, folded it neatly over the back of the chair. He fingered his shirt cuffs unhurriedly before sitting down and carefully removing the plastic lid on his cup. All the while Carey felt the same fidgety dread he had back in prenuptial counselling when it had seemed to take the Reverend forever to formulate what he was going to say—mingled now with fury. Then Carey remembered *what* the Reverend had said: the Reverend, bless his heart, had tried to warn him.

"Betty says you're all very excited. It's March, right?"

"What?"

"When the baby comes. Your life is about to change forever. What a wonderful thing. And remember, we still do christenings."

"Can I ask your advice about something, Reverend?"

"Please," he said. "And please call me Brian."

"Brian. It's about a friend of mine. He's in a—well, it's a similar situation, but it's not me. I mean—" Carey snapped his biscotti in half. "I met him at the childbirth class we're taking. His wife is pregnant too."

Reverend Chalmer, Brian, leaned back in the chair, listening.

"The thing is, his wife is going to have a baby, but the baby isn't his."

The Reverend's delicate brows jerked upward.

"The baby isn't his," Carey said again.

"You mean his wife had relations with another man and became pregnant?"

"Yes."

"How does he know this?"

"What?"

"How does he know the baby isn't his? Even if his wife had relations with another man, the baby could still be your friend's."

"It isn't. They weren't—" He took a sip of coffee. "They weren't having relations. That's what he told me."

"Oh," said the Reverend, sounding pained. He looked out the window.

"What should he do?"

"There's a child involved. I advise forgiveness."

Carey bristled. "But she did this and now she acts like nothing is the matter! She won't even admit to it!"

The Reverend appeared to stall between a shake of his head and a nod. "It's a difficult situation, I agree, but I still recommend forgiveness for the sake of the child. And counselling, of course."

"Don't you do annulments anymore?" Carey asked, sarcastic.

"That's the Catholics." The Reverend opened his hands. "There's divorce."

One night Carey screamed so long and loud at Anna that a blood vessel exploded in his nose. A gory bib down his sweater front, he pinched his nostrils and threw his head back and let Anna lead him to the bathroom. While he sat on the tub's edge, she washed the sticky blood off his face and neck. "Why?" he begged her, grabbing the hand that held the cloth. "Why did you do this to me?"

"I didn't do anything. You were the one yelling."

"That's not what I mean. I'll never forgive you, you know."

"It's just a nosebleed," Anna tsked.

He wondered then, he seriously wondered, if she was even right in the head.

When he ran into the Reverend earlier that week, he'd been about to search the classifieds for an apartment. What had stopped him from doing so before was shame. He was so ashamed. If he left Anna, people would ask her why. Betty would certainly ask, and Pauline. One question would lead to another and before long everyone would know that their marriage had remained unconsummated. He would be blamed, of course. The man always was. As Anna's condition grew more obvious, the situation became intolerable; the taunt, in effect, was worse now than his shame. He couldn't live with Anna another minute. After the Reverend left Starbucks, though, Carey didn't pick up the paper again. He drank his coffee reflecting on what the Reverend had said.

The next day he told his students, half in pantomime, that his wife was pregnant. He thought it might help him if he admitted to it, but their jubilant congratulations only embarrassed him and he immediately wished he hadn't. Worse, a few days later he came in and found a large, flattish, rectangular box covering the whole desktop. Crowding around, they insisted that he open it. "For your will be born baby," read the card.

"Oh, fuck," Carey groaned and they understood because swear words are the first words everybody learns.

He tore off the paper. Inside was a crib. He could barely stammer thank you. So moved was he by their generosity that he took on their inarticulacy. Most of them had arrived here penniless from the desperate places they had fled. They were a Bosnian couple, several Kurds from Iraq, a six-foot Sudanese, three Afghan women in head scarves, a Burmese, and a stunned little Sri Lankan girl with a bindi and only one pronoun. Their own children had fallen asleep to the lullaby of war, but for their teacher's child they wished something safe, new and white with a vinyl-covered mattress and bars the regulation distance apart. Humbled as well as touched, Carey tried to think of something he might have done and felt proud of, but he couldn't see past how he'd been torturing Anna. He'd always thought of himself as a nice guy. Everyone did. Maybe the Reverend was right. Maybe it was time to turn the other cheek. He didn't think the marriage could be saved, but at least he might salvage his dignity.

He was careful entering the apartment when he came in that afternoon. "Anna?" he called, to no reply. But where lurked Smitty? In what corner crouched the striped and splay-foot beast? Carey slid the box along the carpeted hall, peering in each doorway before he passed it. In the bathroom, the litter box brimmed with abstract figurines of desiccated shit, but the deceivingly unforked tail was nowhere to be seen.

In the nursery, he took all the pieces out of the box, was staring perplexedly at the instruction sheet and the little plastic bag of bolts when the phone rang. He answered in the bedroom. It was Pauline, his sister-in-law. Instantly, Carey became ticky and nervous. Pauline had his number, he was certain—maybe Anna had given it to her! She had his number, and now she was calling him.

He said, "Anna's not here. I think she's at your mother's."

"She is. I'm here too, and I just found out that she hasn't had an ultrasound." There was a pause in which Carey assumed he was to offer an explanation for this outrageous omission. With none forthcoming, Pauline went on. "I mean, she's seven months pregnant and she hasn't had an ultrasound."

"She goes to a naturopath."

"That's what I just found out. A naturopath? Give me a break. You could have a baby with two heads. You realize that, don't you? Do you want a baby with two heads?"

"No," said Carey, sitting down on the bed. That would be a dead giveaway. Nervously, he began tweaking at his glans through the fabric of his pants.

"Well?" Pauline demanded.

"Who's the father?" Carey blurted.

"Why do you all keep asking me that? It isn't funny anymore."

He hung up. Everything had changed colour in the room, the walls washed with a rosy hue as if he were squeezing a bulb that pumped blood to his eyes, tinting his vision. Then the overhead projector in his mind switched on and the little Sri Lankan girl in his class appeared before him stained, not red, but with the cosmetic yellow dye she sometimes used. His whole fist filled up, plenty rising out the top too, so there was nothing the matter with him physically.

First Anna's belly came home, then, a full moment later, the rest of her. She was rubbing the small of her back and smiling to herself. When she saw him there, she looked taken aback. Carey, who made a point of never acknowledging the martyr-like pleasure she took in her discomfort, said nothing by way of greeting, merely continued planning his next day's lesson on the coffee table.

"Maybe I'll take a bath before dinner," she told him.

She had to lumber past the nursery on her way to the bathroom but didn't look in. Carey heard the tub filling and the porcelain squeak complainingly as she lowered her bulk in. He went to turn on the nursery light, pausing in the hall. The water swished and plashed in rhythm, then Anna's voice started up, resonant in the echo chamber of the bathroom, sounding like more than one singer, like two overlapping in the slow round of a lullaby. For a long time he stood transfixed.

The sound of scratching brought him to and he stepped away from the bathroom door. He followed it to the source: the bottom cupboard in the kitchen where Anna kept the canned goods. Smitty. He grazed his fingernails across the wood.

From inside, a frenzied tearing.

When Anna called to him, he went right away, found her in the nursery clutching a towel that would barely close around her. She gestured to the assembled crib sitting alone in the middle of the room. "Did you do this?"

He took all the credit. "Yes."

"Oh, Carey," she sighed.

Seeing she was about to cry, Carey opened up his arms. Then Anna let out a little shriek as something gushed from between her thickened legs. Instantly, the carpet sopped it up, but they both stood blinking down at the lily pad of wetness.

"Was that pee?" Carey asked.

"Archie gets up at seven-thirty." He pointed to the picture strip thrown against the wall by the overhead projector. "He takes a shower. He eats breakfast. He reads the paper." It was the kind of day Carey would have liked to have himself, the kind of life—in black-and-white, in present habitual, securely routine, devoid of surprises. "At eight-thirty, he drives to work. He starts work at nine o'clock." At no point in Archie's day did his wife's waters break because, unlike Carey, Archie didn't have a cartoon marriage.

A knock on the classroom door. Carey opened it to the security guard handing him a note. Anna had gone to the hospital. He folded the paper in half and, slipping it in his shirt pocket, resumed teaching.

"At noon, he eats lunch in the cafeteria."

At noon, Carey went downstairs and ate his sandwich in the staff room.

In the afternoon, the security guard came back with a note that this time asked him to phone the hospital. "It's an emergency."

His students were still barely able to chorus back the mundane events of Archie's day. Carey told the security guard, rather shortly, "I'm in the middle of a lesson."

After class, he did his photocopying for the next day and put order to his desk as it seemed likely that he'd have to call a substitute. He wandered out to the parking lot, then sat a long time in the car as if trying to recall how to start it. "At four o'clock, Carey drives home," he said, turning on the ignition.

Two blocks from school, he passed a bus stop and saw from the corner of his eye the little Sri Lankan girl waiting. "What would Archie do?" he asked himself as he looped around the block. Archie's inky hair never moved. He was entirely composed of lines.

Archie, an affable smile penned across his face, would offer her a ride.

When he pulled up, it took the girl a moment to notice it was her teacher leaning across the passenger seat to open the door. "Rajeswary!" he called. Shyly, she came over jingling the little bells on the anklets she wore above her Nikes, giggling helplessly.

"Your bus no coming," she sang.

"*My* bus," Carey corrected. "Where do you live? I'll drive you home." He patted the seat and grinned right at her bindi. "What's your address?"

She told him, painstakingly chanting it as he'd taught her.

"Do you live with your parents?" Carey asked as they drove off.

Her huge uncomprehending eyes turned to him.

"Your mother and your father."

"Oh," she said, frowning. "Your mother dead."

He received this news with a giddy, "What?" His mother *dead*?

"War," said Rajeswary. "Your mother dead."

Disappointment. For several minutes he drove in sour silence, eastward, past muffler shops and dollar stores and produce markets. Finally the girl spoke again. "Your baby?"

"*My* baby?" he said in a mocking tone. "*My* baby?"

"*My* baby!" she shrieked, embarrassed. He had sunk into a funk she couldn't understand. "Your happy," she told him.

"Am I?" he shouted at her.

"Yes! Your father!"

He sneered.

"Your address," she whimpered.

"Here?" He stopped the car in front of a coin laundry where, on the second storey, apartment windows faced the street. Even after the frightened girl had bolted from the car, Carey sat there pounding his fist against the steering wheel. He'd racked his brain! Night after night he'd lain awake trying to think of the men Anna knew who might be responsible, but he hadn't been able to think of anyone. He half suspected she was pregnant with an elaborate lie.

With a screech he drove off homeward. Surely by now it would be over. Surely he wouldn't have to watch.

When he got in, the answering machine was winking its red, accusing eye. There was a single, hissing message that left him stunned. "Asshole," Pauline said. "There is no heartbeat."

He went and stood in the nursery door, staring in at the crib in the centre of the otherwise empty room. Tucked up inside it, a bolus of grey fur.

## The Unexpected

The tyrant was dying; she would not moon about to watch. Anna and her mother could stare at him in his cage of pain, but not Pauline. She got a standby flight to Acapulco and from there took the bus. Took buses. Often she was the only *gringa* on them. The men crowded around her, clicking and whistling like starlings. The only English phrase she heard was, "Hey, Blondie." At first she didn't realize they meant her.

Almost immediately she found herself seduced. It was the fruit. The mango's hairy core as she sucked it reminded her of a Mound of Venus. So like the women's fallen breasts were the papaya, their seeds slippery, cum-coated. She bounced on the seat while the huge breasts of the peasant woman next to her, unrestrained by a brassiere, moved in the same orgiastic rhythm. The dark oily faces of the men with their ripe lips began to excite rather than repel her. When she went up to the driver it was partly to feel their cockroach eyes scurrying across her body as she pitched and swayed in the aisle. She gestured for him to stop the bus: too much fruit, too much fruit! He understood and, though they were driving through forest, did not apply the brake until they had passed the sheltering trees and come to a mile of field. She clambered down and, with nowhere to go for privacy, squatted in the ditch. A hot flux gushed exquisitely from her. Glancing back at the bus windows lined with faces, she giggled.

Outside the depot in Oaxaca she bought strawberries for the last part of the trip. Their juice ran down her arms. Nothing to wipe it off with, she had to use her tongue. It was unseemly, she knew, a woman cleaning her arms like a predator after the kill. The men stared on, licking her with their eyes.

"You shouldn't eat those," someone across the aisle said. "You shouldn't eat anything that's not cooked or peeled."

She'd thought he was Mexican, but now that he had given himself away, she noticed his pallor. His accent was American. "The weirdest goddamn thing just happened to me," he told her, "so please don't eat those strawberries."

He had been working in the mountains on a development project, was heading back there now, though the way he was feeling he wasn't sure he would make it. Eight months in poverty and isolation had not agreed with his bowels. He'd lost weight steadily until the morning he knew he had to leave. Something wasn't right. "I had that, you know, gut feeling, ha ha." They got him on the Oaxaca bus, but he had to keep asking the driver to stop.

"I know, I know," said Pauline. "And everybody watched."

"I wondered what the hell could be coming out. I mean, I wasn't eating anything. There I was, hunkering. I looked and—whoa there! Whoa just a minute! A piece of my goddamn intestine!"

"What?" cried Pauline, recoiling. "Coming out?"

"I was shitting out my guts."

"No way."

"Yeah. So I stuffed it back in and got back on the bus gripping my ass. Days it seemed to take to get to Oaxaca. Months. The whole time I sat there clenching."

"Oh, God," said Pauline. "Oh, my God."

"Finally, I got to the clinic. My guts are coming out! My guts are coming out! Crazy *gringo*. The doctor saw me right away. No rubber glove, nothing. Just stuffed his finger up my Khyber Pass. *Señor*, he said with perfect manners, I suggest you go right now to the toilet."

His white face sheening with sweat, he paused and stretched his lips in a slow, sick grimace.

"Are you okay now?" Pauline asked.

"It was as long as my arm. Jesus Christ. Have you ever *seen* a tapeworm?"

She got off the bus at Puerto Ángel and from there had to walk, not on a road exactly, just a wide sandy path through the forested hills where the peasants drove their burros. Whenever she met a man he would, in a simultaneous gesture, avert his eyes and touch his hat brim. So unlike how they had treated her on the buses, either they feared her here or they hated her. She preferred the obscene chirrings because she understood them.

Rounding a bend and looking down: a radiant half circle of sand cupping turquoise water. Where she stayed there were no walls, only a palm-thatched roof supported by wooden posts—a house undressed, in effect. Everything was owned by Americans and most of the people were American or German. The only time she ever saw a Mexican on that beach was very early one morning before anyone else had gotten up. He was utterly still, poised, something shiny in his hand. Walking toward him, she saw it was a machete, but had no time to feel afraid; as soon as he saw her coming, he turned and ran. When she reached the place he'd been standing she noticed a giant sea tortoise a few feet away, labouring, moving her clumsy flippers back and forth in the white sand, making an angel that would ease her down to a depth safe enough to lay her eggs.

The waves rolled onto the beach, then retreated—a rhythm as regular as a metronome set on largo. It was the very pace of life, the timing of those days. She rose early, took a walk, then climbed the hill to the café for breakfast. Afterward, she would lie on the sand reading a book she'd picked up somewhere. Maybe the story didn't interest her, or the sun was glaring off the page, but she found herself always reading the same six pages over and over again. She'd doze off, only to wake in time for a siesta and stagger back to her hammock under the leafy roof. For dinner there was beer, fried fish, fruit. It got dark early. Someone had a guitar and would play Dylan or the Eagles. The pot was excellent. The waves rolled up. The waves rolled back.

She had no idea how long she'd been there when she began to feel unwell. There was no way of telling time, no calendar or clock. Too much of an effort, carving notches in a tree. No one had a mirror so she couldn't tell if her hair had finally bleached enough to earn her the appellation Blondie, or if the skin on her bare ass had darkened to a native shade. Her body offered no clues at all; since she'd gone off the pill, her periods had ceased. Civilization's other chronometer, laundry day, did not apply.

"I ate some strawberries," she confessed when someone finally noticed she was ill. Apparently it was common knowledge that the fields were irrigated with raw sewage. She mentioned the possibility of worms.

"Worms at least."

She should have gone back to Puerto Ángel and found a doctor, but couldn't face the walk. Even getting from her hammock to the beach exhausted her. She would lie in a stupor on the sand, now and then digging a hole to retch in, thinking about her father who would be dead by now. Probably she was sunstruck from lying there too long, delirious and therefore susceptible to weird imaginings. Her father had died, but that did not mean the end of their clash of wills. Far from it. Now he was inside her, fighting her from within.

Then one morning she woke feeling herself again, but very hungry. Overnight her energy had returned. Triumphant, she climbed the hill to the café. The woman who worked there looked surprised to see her. "You haven't been around for so long, I thought you'd split."

"How long?" asked Pauline.

The woman shrugged, guessing. "Six weeks?"

It had seemed a lot longer to Pauline, who now felt silly for imagining the spirit of her father had possessed her in the guise of a tapeworm. She must have been hallucinating. In fact, she remembered she'd eaten some mushrooms a few days before falling sick, so maybe the whole episode had been nothing more than a very long, very bad trip. She ordered a *café con leche* and pancakes. The woman sauntered over to the wood stove. Dangling between her brown thighs, the pink string of a tampon.

The waves rolled on. She sang "Tequila Sunrise" again and passed along the joint. Leaning back into the arms of some boy, she heard him whisper, "*Gorda,*" felt his tongue work through her tangled hair and probe her none too clean ear. Just then, something lurched in her belly. She sat up, rose clumsily to her feet and hurried from their circle with the boy in tow.

"*Qué pasa?*" he asked.

"Leave me alone."

"Is it because I called you fat?"

"Get lost," she told him. She could feel it coiling and uncoiling, nudging the walls of her gut, slithering through the folded corridors of intestine, trying doors. She pounded fists against her spongy, distended abdomen. "Get lost!"

Putting on her clothes the next morning confirmed that she was bloated. Her shorts would not close. Thankfully, she had a drawstring skirt and a baggy shirt. Clutching her phrase book, she left Paradise, not even wearing any panties.

There was no translation for "tapeworm," she discovered after arriving at the Puerto Ángel clinic. *"Serpiente,"* she told the nurse, *"serpiente,"* and pointed to her ass.

*"Loca,"* she heard the nurse tell the doctor in the next room. *"Otra gringa loca."*

*"¿Esta vestida?"* asked the doctor. They both laughed, then the nurse came back with a half-dozen white suppository bullets that were, naturally, ineffective.

All her life Pauline had watched people watching her sister. She had seen their eyes shift focus the moment Anna came into the room and never really centre back on Pauline. They would look to Pauline again, certainly, but their eyes would be empty after that, gazing inwardly instead, at the lovely memory of Anna passing. Didn't Pauline want to claw at those eyes every time that happened? Didn't she just want to scream? It wasn't fair and neither was how Pauline was blamed for every fight between the sisters. So many weekends grounded for supposedly picking on Anna, Pauline seemed to have spent the whole of her adolescence in the prison of her room. Of course, Pauline was also punished for the many outrageous things she did. She was known as an attention-seeker, though attention wasn't half of what she sought. What she really wanted was to be adored, like Anna.

In Mexico, as she moved over the hot sand, stately, one—no, two—in a procession, everyone turned to follow her with their eyes. There were astonished double takes, audible clucks of admiration. Strangers patted her belly, stroked it even, despite the nudist credo not to touch without permission. They would not let her be alone, not even for a second. If she rose from her hammock and headed toward the waves, someone would instantly appear on either side to escort her in. They took turns fanning her with palm fronds and once, while she napped on the beach, someone sculpted her likeness in wet sand three feet away. Waking, she marvelled at the belly of the sand goddess beside her, the protruding navel a seashell spiral. If only it could have lasted.

She came home before she got too big to fly. The next week she had the ultrasound. "Look," said the technician, pressing the lubricated wand hard under Pauline's ribs. On the screen, the ghost of five little bean-shaped toes curled and uncurled.

"Great," Pauline drawled. "It has a foot." Nothing could convince her that these separate parts would come out properly strung together. No way. Pauline had done too many drugs. She planned donations to the eye bank and the foot repository after it was over.

"You don't want the baby?" asked the technician.

"I'm more of a cat person," Pauline admitted.

They offered her a picture, so she took the one of the foot and brought it home to show her mother. Betty surprised her by saying, "It's too bad your father couldn't see this."

"Why? He'd only ground me."

"He wouldn't have to. That baby's going to ground you. You'd better believe it."

Pauline didn't. Nobody had ever really cramped her style, and a person weighing in at under ten pounds was, she thought, an unlikely first.

"I'm dying!" she screamed. She was pushing a planet out her loins in great shuddering, tearing waves. "I'm dying!" And finally a head emerged, then a floppy sunburned body gooey with silver vernix. Eyes slitty, but the mouth open wide. Inside: white gums and a furred, thrushy tongue that would soon shoot burning darts up Pauline's milk ducts. The greedy way she grabbed at the nipple the moment she was placed on Pauline's chest gave Pauline her first inkling as to how things were going to be. They were going to be about the baby. Already the baby was shrieking *Me! me! me!*

They sent her home the next day. How to care for an infant, Pauline had no idea. Every time they'd wheeled Rebecca into the room in her clear plastic box, Pauline had opened one eye and waved the nurse off as if refusing the fare on a dim sum trolley. She hadn't wanted to see anyone who could have used her so violently.

Once home, she hobbled around the house with a sopping, brick-thick menstrual pad between her legs, but no one paid attention. "I have a hemorrhoid," she announced to Anna and Carey and Betty convening around the bassinet. Betty was concerned because Rebecca had changed colour and now looked washed in an iodine solution. All over her misshapen head, black hair was patched like a radiation victim's. Pauline lifted the hand mirror and examined the Catherine wheel of broken blood vessels in her left eye, from pushing. No one had given her an ounce of sympathy for that either.

She'd had enough. She was going back to Mexico with her inheritance. Bowlegged, she pegged up the stairs, dressed, packed and left unnoticed. She thought she would call a cab from the grocery store on the corner, but when she had got halfway across the yard *Me! me! me!* came floating through the open window. *Me! me! me!* Panic overwhelmed her. She beat a stinging retreat and burst back in the house.

"Is she crying?" she called.

"Shh!" hissed Anna. "You're going to wake her up!"

In Pauline's nightmare she was watching herself sleep. For hour after decadently uninterrupted hour, she slept on because, for once, Rebecca was not shrilling. She watched herself toss dreamily in the covers, saw her own chest heave languorous sighs of relaxation and peace. The dream-Pauline was not the one having the nightmare. She was in a state of complete bliss.

Then, in the nightmare, the closed bedroom door opened up a crack. Someone was looking in at the dream-Pauline, but she didn't know it. The door opened wider and a person stepped inside. For some reason the diminutive stature of the intruder was the most terrifying thing about her. She was an evil imp or dwarf or, worse—a child! Reminded then that there was a baby in the house, Pauline began to panic. Where was the baby? Why wasn't she waking every other hour? And who was this menacing little creature creeping over to the bed, tiptoeing closer and closer to her oblivious dreaming self? Had she done something to the baby? What? What?

Now it became apparent that it *was* a child, a child dressed up like a lamb. Still Pauline didn't wake, not until the child was right beside her, glowering in her fleece hood, ears pricked up. Abruptly, the dream-Pauline sat up, pulling the covers tight around her. Her mouth opened to scream, but no sound came. Only the little girl could speak. She grabbed Pauline's wrist.

"Me-ow."

"I'm in labour!" sang Anna on the phone.

"Right," Pauline scoffed.

"I *am*!"

"It's false labour."

"My waters broke."

Pauline hesitated. After seven months of jealous waiting, she was unwilling to let her hopes rise, especially prematurely like this. "Any contractions?"

"What do they feel like?"

Pauline laughed. "Call me back."

*Pleased to Meet You*

The day before, the sisters had gone for lunch. Two men in business suits, allowed now to perform all the chivalrous gestures banned by feminism, rushed to open the door for Anna. They followed her solicitously into the restaurant, leaving Pauline outside grappling with a toddler, the full set of luggage that came with her—diaper bag, toy bag, food bag, stroller—and now the door. Pauline nearly spat. How she longed for that commanding, dirigible figure herself! She wanted to feel once again inflated with her own euphoria.

Rebecca was in the bathroom unspooling toilet paper all over the floor. "Auntie Anna's going to have a baby. Baby's coming." She scooped up her child, hot sticky cheek against her dry one, cool seashell ear. "Poor Auntie Anna," she laughed. Soon she would be as enslaved by a tiny pair of hands creased at the wrists—screw-on hands!—by a round tyrant face peeking out from under a KKK-hooded bath towel. Unbidden and unstoppable, the love would pour out of her like milk.

Anna didn't call back until the next morning when she was about to leave for the hospital. Pauline said she would meet her there. By cab, she took Rebecca to her mother's where, parting, she grabbed her dirty hand, kissed it fervently, then pushed it right inside her mouth, pretending to eat it. Rebecca shrieked with delight. *If anything happens to you,* Pauline incanted in her head, *I will kill myself by the slowest, most agonizing method. I will stick pins in my every pore. I will gargle battery acid.*

Anna had just been relegated to a curtained cubicle when Pauline arrived. "Where's Carey?"

"He's working," said Anna. "But he'll come. I know he will."

"If you've actually got a father, he may as well be here."

Anna bowed her head and, gripping the chrome bed rails, panted heavily. When she lifted her face again, Pauline saw how bloated she was, her pretty features embedded in flushed and sweaty cheeks. "I feel like pushing," she gasped.

"What? Already?" Pauline hurried off to get a nurse.

The nurse came back with Pauline and did the internal examination while Pauline stayed by the head of the bed. "You're not the teeniest bit dilated," she told Anna as she peeled off the rubber glove. "I'm going to send you home."

"No!" cried Anna. "The baby's coming!"

"That may be," said the nurse, "but it's not coming soon."

"I won't go home! I won't!" She flopped sideways on the bed and curled up, hiding her face so it was hard to tell if she was crying or puffing through another contraction. The hospital gown stretched open between the ties and Pauline looked away with a smile. Anna was huge. It would take her years to shed that weight.

The nurse said, "You'll be more comfortable at home."

"We can go to Ma's," Pauline suggested.

"No!"

The nurse turned to Pauline. "I'll get the resident to come and see her."

As soon as she had gone, Anna asked plaintively, "Paulie? How bad is it going to get?"

"Awful," Pauline chirped.

Anna reached for her hand and, embarrassed, Pauline gave it to her and let her squeeze it. Twenty minutes later the resident finally showed. He was not bad-looking, blond with wire-framed glasses, but Pauline decided—nobly, she thought—that this was not the time. He asked Anna to roll over onto her back and, with her permission, lifted the gown. He had brought a fetal heart monitor which he placed on one side of Anna's belly. Immediately it broadcast her digestive rumblings across the room. He moved it around: more underwater churnings. Pauline was staring at the oddity of Anna's navel, which had not popped but was instead a deep hole with no visible bottom. When she looked up, she saw the resident had fixed on her a look so sobering that she no longer found him remotely attractive.

"I have a phone call to make," she announced, wresting her hand from Anna's, hoping she didn't sound too panicky. "I'll be back."

She walked quickly past the nursing station. She was thinking how, when she had first got back from Mexico, her mother had accused her of having no conscience. "Your father died without being able to tell you goodbye. Couldn't you even have called?" Pauline had retorted, "There wasn't a phone!" No one understood that it was out of respect for Robert that she'd stayed away.

She found the bathroom and, once inside, began to sob. Remorse gushed out of her—her!—former perpetrator of so many childhood atrocities, outlandish denier of them. She used to bury Anna's dolls in the garden, marking the spot with a cross of sticks. As soon as Anna discovered one missing, she would run shrieking into the yard to find the grave and disinter it. Once, the night before school pictures, Pauline cut off one of Anna's braids. Though Anna always went to Robert demanding justice, Pauline stubbornly refused to acknowledge her guilt. The golden snake of Anna's braid in her own wastebasket, still Pauline wouldn't confess. Yet she *had* done those things and, sobbing over the sink, she couldn't shake the hideous feeling that she was also at fault for whatever had gone wrong with Anna's baby, though it was a tragedy she would not have wished even on her worst enemy.

As soon as she had pulled herself together, she went to phone Betty. "Ma," was all she managed to say. "Oh, Ma."

"Has something happened?"

"Ma, it's dead."

Pauline had never known her mother to cry. What she heard now, once she finally managed to quiet herself, was a pause, a metallic rasp and click, an inhalation, then the quiet pop of the filter released.

"I better phone Carey."

"Isn't he there?" Betty exclaimed.

Pauline left a message for him at home. She looked in the phone book for the school where he worked, but none of the names sounded familiar. She went to the gift shop for more quarters, then called around until she found the right place. When she got back to the ward, she couldn't find Anna's cubicle. She looked in one, then the next, but behind every curtain a different woman was abandoning her breathing exercises. Frantic now, she returned to the nursing station just as the nurse who had done the internal examination rounded the corner.

"They're taking your sister upstairs," she said, gesturing down the corridor.

"What about the baby?" cried Pauline.

"What?"

"The baby!"

"Didn't the resident speak with you?"

"No."

"You'd better go with her."

"Where are they taking her?"

"Up to Psychiatry. You can catch up. Go."

Pauline ran. Turning at the end of the corridor, she saw a stretcher being wheeled into the elevator. She sprinted and stopped the door just in time. Anna was sobbing on the stretcher while the other people in the elevator, the orderly, a man on crutches, a couple bearing flowers, looked down at her with pity and concern.

"What's going on?" Pauline demanded.

Anna only sobbed louder.

"Tell me what is going on!"

"They won't let me have my baby!"

Pauline reached out. Anna's belly yielded passively to the jab. "Oh you!" Pauline cried, fingers sinking into fat. She brisked her knuckles hard across Anna's forehead.

"Ow!" shrieked Anna, bringing up her hands.

"Hey, hey!" said the man on crutches. The orderly tried to grab Pauline's arm, but she got one last noogie in before the elevator door opened and she burst out. Nearly colliding with a wheel-chair, she flew off down the hall, light on her feet—unlike Anna! She skipped to dodge a cart. "Whoops!"

The taste of sorry had completely left her mouth.

# Acknowledgements

Thank you to —

the gifted Ingrid MacDonald for the graphic,

Allison Matichuck, Zsuzsi Gartner, Annabel Lyon, Louise Young, Morna McLeod, and Helen Soderholm, who read early drafts and did not mince words,

Denes Devenyi and Michael Wilson, who generously lent me stories that, though recognizable here, are no longer about them,

Patrick Crean, John Metcalf and Jackie Kaiser for their enthusiasm and support,

the Adderson and Sweeney families for everything,

Patrick and Bruce for the love.